Alexander Ford was born in 1977 in the peaceful seaside town of Swanage in Dorset and still resides there today with his faithful feline sidekick, Wesley. He has been writing stories of a fantastical nature from a very young age and has often been accused of having a 'vivid imagination'. Through the written word, he has created worlds both better and worse than our own. He invites you to step into one of those worlds and to lose yourself within the shadows of the pages beyond.

Final Age
""Conversations With A Spider"

Also by Alexander Ford

Final Age: A Child's Eye

Alexander Ford

Final Age
"Conversations With A Spider"

Vanguard Press

Timeline

In the year 2024, the world was engulfed by a solar flare, which levelled hundreds of cities and triggered a terrible worldwide pandemic. The outbreak came to be known as the 'Grey-Maw plague'. In the wake of the event, there were global shortages of food, water and power. There were also reports of the world's flora and fauna suffering widespread mutation. After a few months, the Grey-Maw disease was almost contained and near-normality resumed. Several million people had lost their lives and when the governments began reconstruction of the cities, they decided to give the newly constructed metropolises a number designation, as the original names held too much heartache for the population. Seeking stability, the world's leaders forged a new United Nations government and as one of their first acts, they instigated a project called the 'Shelter-Corp initiative'. The government invested heavily in the corporation and bunkers were constructed throughout the world to protect the population. The UN assured the world that they would research all possible future threats to mankind.

In September 2028, a second solar flare ravaged the world. The results were just as devastating as those of the first and the Grey-Maw plague mutated into something even deadlier. While the television and radio stations could continue transmitting, they referred to it as the 'Damocles virus'. The disease irrevocably changed the living and the dead into decaying monstrosities, which could transmit the illness to others via their blood or saliva. The virus was declared a hundred per cent contagious and a hundred per cent deadly; no one appeared to be safe. Many tried to flee the cities, while others remained in their homes and prayed for a rescue that would never come.

It was now thirty-five days after the event...

Chapter One

"Life Lessons"

It moved unseen across the barren hills and watched intently as the motor vehicle appeared on the distant horizon. The target had been sighted.

The warm winds blasted against his gaunt face as he tore along the open highway. From the speeding motorcycle, Spider surveyed the desolate wastelands that lay either side of the seemingly endless road before him. The town of Shadowvale was far behind and he felt a small measure of satisfaction for Michael, now that the boy had a place to call home. In truth it had been an ordeal for him to remain around those people for so long. Grim memories from his past never ceased from playing in his head, constantly provoking a deep rooted desire to inflict pain upon others. Where most would see families and friends, he saw only cattle waiting to be carved. Although his twisted perception of people extended to children, he rarely harmed them. This was largely due to the teachings his grandmother had imparted to him as a child. Apart from when his sadistic side took hold, he had come to perceive life with a cold logic and did whatever was necessary to continue his existence, without any concerns for morality. As he continued to cruise along the highway, his mind drifted back to his youth.

It had been just another day at school, within the small Swedish city of Strömstad and it was nearing the time to return home. The young, blond-haired boy sat at his desk writing up the simple science experiments he had just finished conducting. While all the other children were working in groups, he had done the work alone. Despite being taller than his classmates, he was shunned by the others and often bullied. Vîggo finished his work, closed his text book and looked around at the other students struggling to complete the experiments. The teacher got up from his seat at the front of the classroom and approached the boy. Vîggo knew it was strange for a seven year old to not have any friends his own age, but in many respects he considered his teacher, Mr Johansson, a kindred spirit. While his classmates had spent their free time playing together, he had often taken the opportunity to have long discussions with the teacher about biology and the other sciences. Mr Johansson put on his thick framed glasses and picked up Vîggo's text book.

The man stroked his bushy moustache as he inspected the boy's work, "Young master Hellstrom, surely you haven't finished all the work already?" Vîggo just nodded and remained quiet.

When the man had concluded marking the boy's work, he put away his glasses and looked down at him. "I must admit, I never expected to find such a sharp mind in one so young. Perhaps I should set something a little more advanced for you next time, hmm?"

Vîggo grinned slightly and as the teacher returned to his desk, a familiar dumpy woman leaned through the classroom door. He instantly recognised the rotund individual as the headmistress and watched the smartly dressed woman bustle in to the room to hand Mr Johansson a note. As his teacher read the message, a look of concern crossed the man's face. The boy then noticed the portly headmistress was looking at him strangely, normally she was quite a jovial person and yet today she looked oddly forlorn.

Mr Johansson looked up at him. "Vîggo, please come with me." The man led him out into the corridor, while the rest of the children were left under the supervision of the headmistress. The man walked beside Vîggo in silence until they reached his office. After unlocking the door, the teacher held it open for him and they both went inside. Although the office was quite small, there was a large bay window at the far side of the room, which gave an impressive view of the city and the distant snow-covered mountains.

The middle aged man sat down at his desk and gestured for Vîggo to take a seat, "There really is no easy way to say this. It seems your parents were involved in a vehicle collision this afternoon. It deeply saddens me to tell you they have both passed away."

Vîggo sat silently in his seat and blinked back the tears welling in his blue eyes. "What will happen to me?"

Mr Johansson offered him a handkerchief to dry his eyes, but the boy declined. "Your only relative we have any record of is your grandmother. She apparently lives in the mountains north of the city. Perhaps you could stay with her?"

"I have never met her," replied the boy quietly, as he stared out of the window at the remote, white-capped mountains.

The man walked around his desk and placed a hand on the boy's shoulder. "I've been told by the authorities I can take you to meet her. Would you like that?" Vîggo looked up at him, with tears running down his cheeks and nodded.

Once Mr Johansson had checked a local map of the mountainous region, they set off together in the teacher's pickup truck. The man became lost in the icy wilderness several times while following the directions to the grandmother's property. After an extensive amount of searching, he managed to find the dirt track road which would lead them further in to the mountains. Even with snow chains fitted to the wheels, the four wheel drive vehicle struggled to climb the treacherous icy slopes. The trail soon led out into a snow-filled valley, which was surrounded by dense woodlands and in the distance they could see white plumes of smoke rising from the chimney of a large wood cabin.

Once the teacher had pulled up outside the lodge, they exited the vehicle and trudged through the banks of white snow to the cabin's front door.

Just as Mr Johansson was about to knock on the door, a woman's voice came from behind them, "Who are you?" They both turned around to find themselves face to face with an old, silver-haired lady. Upon seeing Vîggo, she immediately stepped up to him, cupped a hand under his chin and seemed to scrutinise his face. Her icy blue eyes sparkled in the fading sunlight, as she gazed curiously into eyes matching her own.

"He is family," stated the woman in a matter of fact way, as she turned her attention to the man beside him. Vîggo noticed that the elderly woman was making his teacher quite nervous and was quite intrigued as to how such a frail old woman could be so unsettling to a man twice her size.

The teacher offered the lady his hand. "I presume you are Vanja Hellstrom?"

"Perhaps," replied the woman cryptically, while scowling at his outstretched hand.

"My name is Marcus Johansson, I'm a teacher and Vîggo here, is one of my students. May we please discuss this inside out of the cold?"

Vanja looked at the shivering boy and responded, "As you wish." When they entered the cabin, both Marcus and Vîggo were quite surprised by what they saw. Although the dwelling only consisted of a single floor, it had three well-decorated rooms. The large room they were now standing in appeared to be both a general living space and a kitchen. Vanja motioned for them to take a seat by the fire and poured each of them some tea from the pot on the wood stove. Once Vanja had sat down with them by the hearth,

Marcus explained the tragic situation that had caused them to find her.

"So my son is dead," said Vanja calmly as she sipped her tea. "I will look after the boy, but he will not be returning to the city."

"What of his education?" protested the man. "Vîggo is one of the brightest children I have ever taught. It would be a terrible shame to let his talents go to waste!"

"I will teach him what he needs to know," responded the woman. "If you insist, you may visit and teach him here. When he is old enough he will be free to choose his own path."

Mr Johansson was clearly unhappy with Vanja's response, but replied, "You are his legal guardian, so if that is your decision, I will visit him three afternoons a week from now on."

"Once a week," snapped Vanja.

"What if I were to come up here to teach one whole day a week, perhaps at weekends?" asked the teacher trying to find a reasonable compromise. "I'm certain you can teach Vîggo a great deal, but surely you want your grandson to have every advantage?"

Vanja's eyes narrowed. "Very well Mr Johansson, as you seem to care so much, you may spend each Sunday tutoring my grandson." Marcus patted the quiet boy on the back as he made his way to leave.

Vanja escorted him to the door and asked, "Can you have their remains brought here?"

Marcus was a little taken aback by her request, but nodded. "I will make the arrangements for you. I hope to see you both in a few days. My condolences again for your loss, madam." After Vîggo's teacher had left, the woman sat down with her grandson by the fire.

"Why do you live up here?" enquired Vîggo.

Vanja smiled at him before replying, "This is where I belong. There is much you can learn here."

The pale boy stared at the woman. "Do I belong here, Grandmother?"

The frail looking lady grinned and pulled out an ornate, blood covered knife from inside her coat. "Time will tell."

The sight of the rising smoke from the road ahead brought the slender man's attention back to the present. He slowed the bike to a halt and inspected his surroundings. The bright orange sun was beginning to sink below the horizon and without a safe place to rest, nightfall would likely bring new dangers. Spider tapped the motorcycle's fuel gauge; he was nearly out of gas and more frustratingly, fatigue was beginning to weigh upon him heavily. He took out the binoculars from his holdall and scoured the highway to ascertain the cause of the billowing smoke. In the distance he could see an overturned school bus and a few other derelict cars. The smoke seemed to be rising from amidst the cluster of vehicles. Spider began wheeling the bike along the road in an effort to conserve fuel and in the hope that whoever, or whatever lay ahead wouldn't hear his approach. With the daylight quickly fading, he could just make out an abandoned taxi cab at the side of the road. One of the vehicle's back doors was hanging open and as he reached the car, a rasping noise sounded from within. When he saw the putrid corpse of an elderly man moving to exit the vehicle's back seat, Spider knocked the bike's kick-stand down to prop up the chopper and calmly lit a cigarette in his mouth.

The Infected's blood-weeping eyes stared at the man hungrily as it struggled to climb out of the taxi. When it saw him walking towards the front of the car, its salivating jaw opened and closed with the anticipation of feeding upon him. Spider took a drag of his cigarette, raised a foot to rest on the outside of the open door and just as the creature emerged from the car, he kicked the door shut. As the door crushed the Infected against the side of the vehicle, he heard the satisfying crunch of bone. The man gave the door another firm kick, causing the decaying creature's body to rupture, spilling its rotten innards on to the ground. He inspected the bleeding mass of rancid flesh caught in the buckled door and smiled. Once he had finished his cigarette, he returned to the motorcycle and continued his journey down the road. As he neared the source of the smoke, he could see a small campfire burning between the derelict vehicles. While Spider considered the merits of moving in to investigate, a woman's scream suddenly sounded from the camp ahead. Leaving his bike out of sight, he crept closer in an attempt to gain a better vantage point. Caught in the orange flickering glow of the fire, he could see the form of a large man writhing on top of a crying teenage girl. Once the man had finished using the naked adolescent, he stood up and redressed himself.

"Shut ya damn mouth, ya whore and put yer clothes back on," said the man in a gruff Irish accent. He laughed as he looked down at the whimpering girl on the ground, "Got a big day for ya tomorrow, me girl. Ya soon be property of the 'Family'." Spider strode purposefully through the darkness towards the camp, with his long black coat trailing behind him. He stopped a few feet away from the rotund man and struck a match to light a cigarette he had just placed in his mouth.

"What the hell do ya want?" whispered the red haired man, who was clearly more than a little rattled by the sudden arrival of the sinister looking individual. Spider took the cigarette from his lips, exhaled smoke and stared at the man.

"I mere-ly wish to make use of your fire," stated Spider in his stilted Swedish accent.

The Irish man drew a gun from his side, "Get out of here, before I decide to blow the head off ya shoulders!"

Spider's dark ringed eyes narrowed as he studied the sawn-off shotgun now being pointed at him, "I can pro-vide you with food if you wish."

"Oh, I could do with a meal! Hand it over then and be on yer way," ordered the obese slaver, now aiming the gun at his head.

"The food is not yet pre-pared and I doubt you wish to waste pre-cious ammo kill-ing me," responded the tall figure calmly.

"Fine, be getting on with it then," said the large man, sounding quite frustrated and gestured to the campfire.

"Who is the young la-dy?" asked Spider, as he collected a few items from the holdall on his back. The Irishman briefly turned to look at the sobbing slave girl lying on the tarmac and in that moment, Spider acted. The distracted man felt a leather gloved hand at his throat, swiftly followed by a piercing sting in the side of his neck. Spider lowered the incapacitated man to the ground and retrieved the hypodermic. Although he had just used the last of the anaesthetic, he deemed the usage justified for what he had planned. The girl lying nearby looked terrified of him and wailed almost constantly. He knew the young woman's cries would likely attract other creatures and Spider considered this unacceptable. After pouring something from a bottle on to a rag, he promptly covered the girl's lower face with the chloroform soaked cloth, rendering her unconscious. Leaving the teenage girl to sleep, he turned his attention back to the slaver.

Night had fallen by the time the Irishman awoke, and he found himself propped up right next to the fire. He was quite alarmed to find he couldn't move, or even turn his head and the stranger was now sat opposite him, with the campfire burning between them.

"The girl is still a-sleep," whispered Spider. "Are you hun-gry?"

The paralysed man's eyes looked down to the fire, where pieces of meat were sizzling in a metal pan, "Why can't I move, damn you!" responded the man hoarsely.

The edges of Spider's mouth curled slightly in to a small smile, "The drug will wear off short-ly."

"The food sure does smell good," said the large man smacking his lips. "I thought you were gonna kill me fer sure."

"No, I will not be kill-ing you," replied Spider as he brought a strip of meat to the man's mouth on the end of his knife. The man struggled to chew the morsel, but he seemed to enjoy the food. The Swedish man fed the slaver a few more mouthfuls and then settled down to eat some himself.

Once he had finished the meal, he said, "It is, an acquired taste."

"What was it, Vermin?" asked the obese man, now a little worried. "Oh no, it wasn't Leecher meat was it?" The gaunt man leant forward into the firelight with his mouth set in a sinister grin and silently gestured to something lying at his side. The sweating Irishman was almost too afraid to look away from the piercing stare of Spider's blue eyes.

When he finally dared to look down at the bloody pile of meat that lay before him, he instantly screamed. Lying in a pool of blood, were the remains of two partially eaten, severed limbs, which the man now recognised as his own arms.

"What have ya done!" shrieked the red haired man as he stared down at the sewn up stumps, where his arms used to be. "You're worse than the bloody family!"

Spider stood up and loomed over the petrified man. "Tell me a-bout the fam-ily and I may a-llow you a quick death."

The sobbing man, who was trying not to vomit, explained that there was a group of survivors, who lived on a farm about a dozen miles down the highway. Apparently they often preyed upon those who travelled the road and they paid well to those who brought them fresh bodies to consume. Spider decided it would be inefficient to kill his captive and in the morning he would pay this 'Family' a visit.

When dawn came, Spider was unconcerned to discover the girl had run away during the night. Upon searching the slaver's bags, he was pleased to find they contained both water supplies and ammunition for his new sawn-off shotgun.

Later that bright and sunny morning, Spider was once more pushing his motorcycle along the open highway. Occasionally he would stop and look back at his armless travelling companion, who was being pulled along by a length of chain around his neck.

It remained hidden from view as it followed the target along the road. They were behind schedule and it had been instructed there could be no further delays.

Chapter Two

"Human Weakness"

The cold rain continued to pour from the dark tempestuous skies and thunder boomed once more overhead. A streak of lightning illuminated the nearby hillside, which was covered by blackened rows of dead trees, stripped bare of their branches. Suspended from the porch's roof beam by lengths of rope, two corpses swayed gently in the wind. Spider stood in the torrential rain looking up at the elderly couple hanging from their recently self-imposed gallows and shook his head in disapproval. With his knife ready in hand, he entered through the front door of the house, dragging his armless companion along after him on a length of chain secured around his neck. Spider knew this was not the 'Family's' farm his unwilling follower had spoken of, but the sudden freezing downpour had forced him to leave the highway to seek shelter.

"I hope ya die of pneumonia, ya bastard", grumbled the soaking wet Irishman. Ignoring the armless man's words and the constant pounding pain in his head, Spider staggered wearily along the hallway. He passed a few photographs of the old couple, who were now hanging from the porch outside and as he gazed at the pictures, the images began to blur. He suddenly felt dizzy and leant against the wall to steady himself. Upon struggling to the kitchen, the shivering man began to search through the cupboards and it became quickly obvious as to why the house's owners had taken their own lives. There was no food or water left here and like many other people, the prospect of facing the horrors outside had been too much to bear. He closed the fridge and caught sight of his reflection in the mirror above the sink. His complexion was sickly white and once more his vision began to blur. After removing one of his gloves, he held the hand to his forehead and was unsurprised to find he was burning up with a fever. When his legs unexpectedly buckled under him, he reached out for the sink, but found he didn't possess the strength to stop his descent to the tiled floor.

"Ha! You've got the virus! Now yer gonna pay asshole!" bellowed the Irishman gleefully, as he rushed forward to stamp on his fallen captor. The gaunt man managed to look up, just as the slaver brought his foot hammering down upon his chest. The blinding pain of the blow shocked Spider briefly back to consciousness and on instinct he reached feebly inside his coat pocket to retrieve something.

The large man knelt down on Spider's throat and roared, "Time to die, ya son of a bitch!" The slaver felt the choking man's hand trying to move under him and laughed, "What yer gonna do, fondle me to death?" The obese man leered over him as he continued to crush down on his throat, but his expression changed to one of confusion as the dying man tried to speak.

Spider sneered at his attacker as he whispered a single word, "Bang."

"What?" responded the man now even more puzzled. The slaver suddenly realised his mistake and his eyes grew wide with terror, in that fleeting moment, Spider grinned.

The Irishman cried, "Wait I-," but his words were cut short by an almighty boom.

The slaver's entire torso was torn asunder by the blast, leaving the fevered Spider lying in a vast pool of blood. He looked up at the dripping guts plastered all over the kitchen walls and then at the smoking sawn-off shotgun in his hand, before slipping in to unconsciousness.

It had been two days since Vîggo's parents had died and their bodies had been delivered that morning to the cabin. The elderly woman stood watching her grandson, as he skinned and prepared two rabbits for their dinner.

"You have a talent for that," commented Vanja.

Vîggo shrugged. "I am just doing what you showed me, Grandmother."

"That is true, but you handle the knife better than I taught you."

"Thank you," replied the boy.

"It was not a compliment, merely an observation," stated the silver-haired woman.

After they had eaten, Vanja took the boy outside, to the rear of the lodge. Before them was a large funeral pyre, made up of dozens of large logs and lying atop it were the bodies of Vîggo's parents.

Vanja turned to him. "Death should not be feared, or mourned. Such feelings are merely sentimental weakness; they are of no use to us."

Vîggo's eyes watered, but he managed not to cry and asked, "Why are we not just burying them?"

"We must burn them first, or else wolves and bears will come to devour their remains."

"Oh", said the boy, now desperately trying to keep that grotesque image out of his head.

"It is just the way of things," stated Vanja. "Both man and beast must often become hunter, or prey during their short lives." His grandmother then lit the pyre and they stood together in silence as the flames began to consume the deceased. Vîggo forced himself to watch as the flesh on his parents' bodies was slowly burned away, to reveal blackened bones.

While gazing in to the fire, he thought about his grandmother's words and whispered to her, "I do not want to be 'prey' anymore."

Vanja smiled. "Then I shall teach you, child." She took him back inside the cabin and sat down next to him. "The first lesson I shall teach you concerns your prey. Unless forced to, we do not kill the young, or the females who carry them. Not only do the infants provide little meat, by depleting their numbers, hunters could potentially cause themselves to starve in seasons to come."

One day a week he received tutoring from Mr Johansson, who largely focused upon the sciences. The teacher remained impressed with the boy's ability to learn and had little doubt Vîggo had a bright future ahead of him. During the other six days of the week, Vanja imparted her considerable knowledge of how to survive, hunt and kill. Under his grandmother's guidance, the young boy quickly became a proficient hunter with the knife and soon began to seek more challenging prey.

"I think he's awake!" exclaimed a young girl.

"What if he's Infected?" asked another female voice.

Spider opened his eyes and winced, as he found the light hurt his eyes. He seemed to be lying bare-chested on a sofa in the living room of the house. He could see his holdall lying near the doorway and his leather coat was on the floor next to him. His head was still throbbing with pain and he remained feverish.

A small, dark haired girl offered him a glass of water. "This is from your bag, I hope you don't mind, me and my sister kinda drunk some of it." Spider was too weak to answer and barely managed to raise his head to sip a few mouthfuls of water, before collapsing once more to the sofa.

"We lit the fire for you," said a smaller girl, pointing at the fireplace.

Spider's brow furrowed with concern and he managed to whisper, "They will see the smoke."

"Don't be silly," said the older girl, who was likely eight or nine years old. "The monsters won't notice the smoke."

"I'm Susie and this is my big Sister Rachel," said the other girl, who was clutching a small, blue teddy bear.

"What sort of meat is that in your bag?" asked Rachel.

The heavily perspiring man weakly answered, "Did you eat it?"

"No! It smelt weird!" said Rachel, sticking out her tongue in disgust. "Anyway, we have some food left, just not much water."

"Go east to, Shadow-vale," whispered Spider, who then began to cough violently. Both the girls looked frightened when his incessant coughing brought forth a trickle of blood from his mouth. The sickly looking man lay on his back gasping for breath for several moments and then went still.

"Is he dead?" asked Susie worriedly.

"No, just exhausted I think," replied her sister. "We should probably let him rest."

Spider was abruptly awoken by the sound of breaking glass in the hallway. It was dark now and he could hear the sound of a car's engine outside. Upon hearing the girls' screams, he tried to rise from the sofa, but found he was still too weak and just fell awkwardly on to the floor. Sensing footsteps approaching the living room door, he slowly rolled himself in to the gap beneath the sofa and remained silent. The door was kicked open and Spider watched as two pairs of legs entered through the doorway. The intruders laughed about what they were going to do to the children and took several items from the room, including his holdall. He could hear the little girls' crying out for help as they were dragged outside and their terrified shrieks caused him to relive a painful memory...

The images played once more in his head; the group of men laughed, as the blood dripping barbed wire tore deeper in to their frail bodies, making them shriek in agony...

Spider rolled out of his hiding place and through sheer force of will he staggered to his feet. As he stood upright and put on his long leather coat, he heard the sound of the vehicle driving away. He stepped over to the window and looked out in to the night, just as the van's headlights turned west onto the highway. Providing the slaver had told him the truth, the 'Family's' farm would probably only be a few miles away, so it seemed likely they had been the intruders. After he checked his coat pockets, all he found was his motorcycle keys, a lighter and a pack of cigarettes. He was quite annoyed to find both his knife and shotgun were missing. He reasoned the girls had probably placed the weapons in his holdall, when they had moved him from the kitchen. Spider walked in to the hall and saw Susie's blue teddy bear lying discarded on the front doorstep. The gaunt man stared at it for a few moments, as if trying to decide something. After placing the stuffed toy in his front pocket, he went to the kitchen.

He immediately noticed the fractured mirror, which had been damaged by the gunshot and carefully pried a long shard of glass free from the frame.

Spider searched through the kitchen drawers and eventually found what he was looking for. Taking the roll of parcel tape, he wrapped it dozens of times around one end of the sharp glass shard and inspected the shiv. Although still weak from the illness, Spider walked outside to his motorbike, started the engine and roared away down the highway, into the night. A lingering echo of the man he had once been, caused him to entertain the thought of rescuing the girls, but he promptly dismissed the notion as sentimental foolishness. The man dearly wanted to hunt down, torture and kill every member of this 'Family', just for the pleasure of watching them die. Logically he knew his chances of survival were slim, but his grandmother had taught him well. He had no fear of death and by dawn they would all be his prey.

Chapter Three

"Hunter & Prey"

With the rainstorm now passed, the night had turned strangely humid and the moon was shining brightly in the starry skies above. The rider was illuminated in the soft glow of the moonlight as he cruised down the highway and upon seeing a light ahead, he brought the speeding motorcycle to a slow halt on the hill top. Spider took a few moments to survey the bridge below, which spanned a wide gorge. Parked almost halfway along the causeway, he could see the headlights of a battered looking campervan, which had a cloud of steam rising from beneath its hood. The distinct wail of baying wolves echoed in the distance and he watched with fascination as dark shapes appeared at the far side of the gorge. The giant beasts howled and bounded across the bridge, straight towards the group of survivors, who had been desperately trying to repair their vehicle. The four figures initially opened fire upon the charging pack, but quickly turned to seek refuge within their van. Although their brief volley of gunshots had felled one of the beasts, the others had not been dissuaded from their attack and the smell of blood in the night air only seemed to drive them on. One of the fleeing survivors was brought down by the ferocious creatures, before his friends had even reached the vehicle. Spider marvelled at the wolves' sheer size and considered the name insufficient, as these impressive creatures appeared to be as large as the bears he had hunted in his homeland. He observed the snarling beasts with intrigue as they ripped the screaming man apart and began to feast on his innards. Only one of the survivors had managed to get inside the van and in apparent panic, he had locked the doors, preventing the others from entering. While a woman pounded on the van, begging for her comrade to open the door, an older man, who appeared to have a huge bushy grey beard, took one look at the 'Howlers' devouring the remains of his fallen friend and rolled under the campervan. From beneath the vehicle, the old man fired his rifle at one of the beasts and by luck, or skill, he inflicted a severe wound, causing it to retreat back across the causeway. The remaining Howler bounded straight for the woman, who was still banging on the door and pleading to be let inside. The monsters vicious jaws snapped forward to bite her legs and quickly dragged its shrieking victim to the ground to be eaten.

Upon seeing his opportunity, Spider kick-started his bike and roared down the hill towards the bridge. As he neared the Howler feeding beside the camper-van, he abruptly applied the front brake and suddenly veered right, causing the hurtling motorcycle to skid sideways. The Howler looked up from eating its kill, just as the careening bike smashed in to it. The brutal impact crushed the beast's body against the rear of the van and Spider was thrown tumbling across the asphalt. He lay winded on his back for a few minutes, before eventually getting up to inspect the blood dripping mess of fur, flesh and bone now plastered across the back of the van.

Spider smiled in approval as he examined his kill and promptly lit up a cigarette. He went to check upon the damage to his bike, but stopped in his tracks when he heard the ominous sound of a gun being cocked behind him.

"I think per-haps you are be-ing a li-ttle un-grate-ful," said the gaunt man as he slowly turned around, with his hands raised in visible surrender.

"Maybe so," said the old man, as he lowered his rifle, "But I don't know you from shit. I already lost two friends today and I aint looking to join 'em." Spider grinned, lowered his hands and took a drag of his cigarette.

A heavily overweight man, with thick glasses unlocked the van door and leaned out nervously and whispered, "Ha-have they gone?"

"Ya damned fool, ya got Tailor killed!" bellowed the old man. "Why didn't ya just open the damn door!"

"I'm sorry, Mr White, I got scared," whined the squeaky-voiced man. "I thought I was going to have a heart attack."

"Ya fat moron, do everyone a favour and jump off the god damn bridge!" Mr White then moved to enter the van and said, "I'm gonna get my head down for a while, you can stay on watch Horace, ya useless sack of crap!"

Once the old man had gone inside, the bewildered oaf noticed Spider standing silently in the darkness and immediately began to panic. "Who-who are you?" Spider stared intently at the fat man and continued to smoke while he considered his next actions.

"I am just pass-ing through. I believe there is a farm just down the road," said Spider pointing at the far side of the bridge. Horace predictably turned to look where he had indicated and suddenly found the man holding a sharp object to his throat.

"Please don't hurt me!" bawled Horace.

Spider whispered in his ear, "Bring me wa-ter and fuel for my bike. If you do this, you 'may' live. Dis-appoint me and I will make sure you die most pain-fully." Horace felt the sting lift from his throat and the stranger backed away, motioning for him to enter the van. While Spider waited for the dim-witted man to bring the requested items, he heaved the chopper upright and upon inspecting it over, was pleased to find the bike was relatively undamaged. A minute later, the sweating Horace returned with a large can of fuel and a bottle of water.

"Sad-ly I do not have su-fficient time to deal with you," said the Swedish man as he began to pour the fuel in to the motorcycle's gas tank.

"Why-why do you talk like that?" blurted Horace nervously.

Spider handed the trembling man the empty fuel can and gave him an incredulous look. "Is my Eng-lish not good?" The terrified Horace struggled to reply and just found himself staring at the malevolent man. Spider's chiselled features and his long hooked nose made the man look oddly ghoulish in the moonlight.

"You over pronounce your words!" exclaimed Horace, eager to break the tense silence.

Spider scowled at the annoying man and replied, "Interest-ing." He then began to speculate upon the best way to kill the bumbling fool.

The van door suddenly opened and Mr White leaned out. "We owe ya for the help, so I can't say I really give a shit about ya taking some fuel and water. Where ya headed anyway?"

"There is a farm near-by, they have my be-long-ings and have also ta-ken some chil-dren pris-oner," said Spider as he flicked the cigarette stub to the tarmac.

Mr White scowled and shook his head, "Damn 'em, ya want a hand?"

Spider grinned. "That would be most help-ful."

After a few minutes of preparation, Mr White was ready to leave with Spider for the farm. He turned to Horace. "Look, fatso, get the van working by the time I'm back, or don't bother being here."

"When-when will you be back?" stammered the ruddy-faced man, squinting through his thick glasses.

"Hopefully by noon tomorrow, now do something right for once and fix the god damn van!"

With Mr White sat on the bike's rear, Spider kick-started the engine and the motorcycle thundered in to life. A cloud of grey smoke suddenly filled the night air, as the rear wheel screeched on the asphalt and they roared away in to the moonlight.

The injured Howler limped along the road and snarled as it sensed the hidden entity. When the huge beast leapt forward to attack, the unseen being lashed out with an arm, effortlessly scything the creature in two. Detecting the target was once more on the move, it increased its speed to follow in pursuit.

During his life, Spider had often found he had more affinity for the older generation, than his own. He found Mr White's brusque manner vaguely reminiscent of his grandmother's demeanour and for that reason he quite liked the man. As he rode on towards the farm, his thoughts once more returned to his childhood.

Seven years had passed since he had first come to live in the mountains and in that time the teenage boy had learnt a great deal from both his teacher and his grandmother. Vîggo had constructed another smaller cabin to use as a place of study and had spent much of his time there of late. On this bright and sunny summer morning, he was eagerly awaiting the arrival of Mr Johansson. When his teacher pulled up outside the lodge in his truck, the excited adolescent raced over to meet the man.

"My goodness, you seem in a good mood this week," commented Marcus as he exited the vehicle. "How did you find the new zoological and medical journals I gave you?"

"They were fascinating and it all makes sense now," exclaimed Vîggo as he brushed his long hair away from his face.

"What do you mean, Vîggo?" asked the man curiously.

"I will show you," responded the tall youth. Marcus followed the young man inside his cabin and put on his glasses to study his surroundings.

"I now have a greater understanding of biology," said Vîggo proudly. Mr Johansson was both shocked and amazed by what was before him. The cabin was adorned by several sturdy wooden tables and upon each of them were a variety of animal carcasses. There were also a number of various spiders in jars on the desks and Marcus could see he had been studying their feeding habits.

"Spiders?" enquired Marcus, raising an eyebrow.

"They are amazing creatures; did you know some species can survive for months at a time, from devouring a single kill?"

The teacher nodded in interest as he examined the remains of the rabbits, wolves and bears that had been carefully dissected. "You have a steady hand my boy, I think you will make a fine doctor or surgeon one day."

Vîggo gave the man a sly smile. "Did you manage to arrange what we discussed?"

Marcus put away his glasses and gave the boy a wide grin. "It's all been arranged, when you're sixteen, you will be attending the Los-Demones state medical college in America."

Vîggo was overjoyed by the news and briefly hugged the man. "This is amazing, but I wonder how my grandmother will feel about it?"

"Providing it is what you truly want, I will accept this as your decision," said Vanja as she walked through the doorway. "I have already taught you much of what I can. You have been an adept student and I could not have wished for a better grandson."

Vîggo found his grandmother's words to be out of character and observed her curiously. When the frail old woman suddenly collapsed, he dashed forward to catch her in his arms. From that day, a doctor came to the cabin daily to check upon Vanja's ailing health. Although she was later diagnosed with an aggressive form of leukaemia, the old woman flatly refused to be admitted to a hospital and from then on Vîggo took it upon himself to do all that he could to care for his grandmother.

In the following months Vîggo watched helplessly, as every day the feisty woman's spirit grew weaker. Twelve months later, she was bedridden and so weak she could barely breathe. Marcus had come this day to pay his respects and was waiting outside her room with Vîggo, while the doctor did what he could to ease her pain. Once the doctor had left, they both entered to sit by her bedside. The formerly fearsome woman looked sickly and was covered with dark bruises, but still smiled when she saw her grandson sitting calmly next to her. Vîggo had taken his grandmother's teachings to heart and showed no sadness as he looked upon the dying woman.

Vanja turned to Marcus. "I thank you for teaching my grandson. I know I have not been kind to you, but it is just my way. Would you please give me my final moments to speak with my grandson alone?"

Mr Johansson nodded and rubbed his eyes, as a tear ran down his face. "It was my pleasure to tutor him madam." Once the man had left the room, Vanja looked back to her grandson.

"I do not have much time," whispered Vanja. "There is one more lesson I may teach you before I am no more." Vîggo's brow furrowed in confusion, he leaned closer and listened intently. The old woman picked up something from beside her bed and offered it to him. Held out before him was Vanja's knife, its sharp edge gleamed in the candlelight and after a moment of hesitation, Vîggo took the sturdy blade from her hands.

"When I am gone, I wish for you to burn my cabin as my pyre," stated the woman.

Vîggo paused before replying, "I will see it is done, but what of this lesson?"

"My grandson, always so eager to learn," chuckled the woman, who then began to cough. "Your great grandfather forged that blade when I was a child and it has served me well for over a lifetime. It has taken many lives and it will take many more I think. I ask you now to spare me the torture of my final hours and pierce this old woman's heart. Let me die."

Vîggo looked into his grandmother's icy blue eyes and could see the torment within. He leaned forward, kissed her on the forehead and pushed the knife point in to her heart, instantly ending her life.

Vîggo said nothing to Mr Johansson when they departed the cabin. He left the home with nothing except his grandmother's knife and the clothes on his back.

The sun was setting and Marcus waited in his truck, as Vîggo entered the cabin one last time. He pulled the smouldering logs from the fire place and threw them to the carpeted floor, instantly starting a small blaze which quickly spread throughout the lodge. The young man walked calmly from the burning building and didn't look back. The hunter had no need of emotion; the hunter had no use for fear. It was time for him to find a new place to belong.

Spider turned off the highway on to a dirt track road and brought the bike to an abrupt halt. In the distance they could see a large farmhouse surrounded by several abandoned vehicles and judging by the plethora of discarded personal belongings lying around, this was the 'Family's' residence. Spider ran a hand through his short blond hair, as he dismounted the motorcycle and then retrieved the shiv from his pocket.

"So what do we do now?" asked Mr White as he readied his rifle.

Spider looked at him deviously and replied, "Now, they die."

The grumpy old man shook his head and sarcastically muttered, "Nice plan."

Chapter Four

"Looking In The Mirror"

Under the light of the moon, the two men surveyed the single storey farmhouse. They watched with interest as a group of men left the residence and climbed into a familiar looking van. Once the vehicle had departed, they turned their eyes back to the building and although there were no obvious signs of life from within, a dim light shone from some of the windows. Just as Mr White was about to speak, two figures walked into view from the rear of the house. The armed men seemed to be patrolling the property, but looked to be caught up in conversation and weren't paying much attention to their surroundings. Spider crouched low as he crept across the dry grassland, to approach them from behind.

Upon seeing his stealthy comrade making his move, Mr White lay low on the hill and trained the sights of his hunting rifle on the two guards.

Spider was now within a few feet of the guards and could smell the rank odour of stale sweat coming from the dishevelled figures. Knowing his fragile shiv would likely be insufficient for the task of killing both the men, he looked to his immediate surroundings for anything that may prove useful. When he caught sight of a short reel of rusty razor wire lying against a nearby fence post, Spider considered the object for a moment and smiled. Using Susie's small teddy bear as padding to protect his palm, he gripped the loop of vicious wire in one hand and readied the shiv in the other. Realising the two men still had their backs turned to him, he rushed forward to strike. He lowered the loop of wire over the left guard's head, down to his bare throat and pulled backwards, while simultaneously raising his left leg to press a foot in to the man's back. The other guard turned to shoot at his attacker, but Spider instantly lashed out with his alternate hand and plunged the glass point of the shiv through his right eye, deep into his skull. With the gaunt man's foot still forced into his upper back, the remaining guard's frantic attempts to free himself proved ineffective and he promptly fell to his knees. As Spider continued to heave on the razor wire with both hands, it cut deeper into the gurgling man's throat, causing a heavy tide of blood to flow from the widening tear in his neck. A distinct crunch sounded as the wire suddenly sheared the man's head from his shoulders, sending Spider stumbling backwards and the headless corpse to drop to the ground.

Mr White had no love for these allegedly cannibalistic kidnappers, but the brutal display he had just witnessed, had left him more than a little fearful of his comrade. With the thought of rescuing the children still in mind, he jogged down the hill and moved up next to the man, who was nonchalantly searching through the dead men's pockets.

Spider passed Mr White a handful of rounds for his rifle and flashed a wicked grin, as he collected a small throwing knife from the decapitated torso.

"Their friends may re-turn. You should re-main on the hill-side," whispered Spider.

"Sure. I can cover ya well enough from up there I guess, but ya need to get those captives out of there, or are ya just here fer the kill'in?" asked Mr White, now wondering if he had made a mistake coming here.

Spider paused in thought and looked at the small blue teddy bear's head poking out of his top pocket. "I will do what I can, but I pro-mise no-thing."

While Mr White returned to the grassy ridge to keep watch, Spider cautiously entered through the front door of the farmhouse. The door opened in to a wooden decked hallway, which was covered in grime and litter. The first rooms he checked were lit by candlelight and seemingly empty, apart from several tattered mattresses lying about the dirty floor. Only one room at the end of the hall had its door closed and he could hear a gruff voice singing from within. He edged slowly through the half-light, towards the door he could now see was marked 'Kitchen', but abruptly stopped in his tracks when he heard another voice muttering beside him. To his right, was a room piled high with bags and standing amidst them was a scrawny man with a mullet haircut, rifling through the various luggage. Despite directly facing him and only being separated by a few feet, the scavenger had not yet seen him skulking in the gloom. Spider reached for the throwing knife in his coat pocket and just as he hurled the blade, his intended target lifted up a suitcase to examine, causing the knife to thud harmlessly in to the luggage. The scavenger looked up at him and beamed a horrid grin, revealing a mouth full of teeth sharpened to fine points.

"Nice try, asshole," said the man as he dropped the bag, to retrieve a pistol from his belt. In that moment, Spider dashed forward to bring an open palm slamming upwards to the underside of the man's nose. The scavenger had no time to react and there was a sickening crunch as the bone was forced up in to his brain. The skinny man stood for a few seconds, staring in to space with blood pouring from his nose and collapsed to the floor. Spider began to search for his belongings amongst the vast pile of bags and after a few minutes of rummaging, he found the dirty black holdall. Hurriedly unzipping the bag, he was relieved to find both the sawn-off shotgun and his knife was still inside. After loading the shotgun, he placed the firearm inside the pocket of his long leather coat. He slung the holdall over his shoulder and with Vanja readied in his hand, he looked about the room. Upon spotting a hatch situated in the corner of the room, he moved over to it and carefully eased it open. There was a flight of stone steps leading down into the darkness and as he quietly descended them, an array of murmuring voices echoed from within.

The air was almost too foul to breathe; it reeked with the stench of decay and excrement. As he neared the bottom of the steps, he could see a small oil lantern hanging from the ceiling; its flickering light bathed the room in a dull orange glow and for the first time in many years Spider found himself revolted by what he saw. The huge stone walled basement, spanned the entire floor of the farmhouse above and caught in the flickering light were several naked men and women chained to the walls. Many of the terrified, emaciated captives had missing limbs, which had been crudely sewn shut and had now begun to rot. Some of the prisoners were clearly too mutilated to escape and frustratingly, there was no sign of Rachel or Susie. The repetitive dull thud of meat being chopped reverberated from somewhere in the gloom and with Vanja in hand, he crept onward into the darkness. Beneath the glow of another oil lantern, he could now see the back of a shirtless, obese figure, who was continually bringing a large meat cleaver down to bear upon a small mangled body. Spider inched forward to gain a better view of the victim and felt a twinge of concern when he saw the body. The heavy blade was cleaving apart the remains of a young child and its hair was black, just like the two girls he had met. The butcher lifted the section of torso from the floor, causing a pile of bloody viscera to slide out from inside the chest cavity and rammed it upon a metal hook, on the end of a suspended chain. While the sweating, stout figure inspected the meat hanging in front of him, Spider silently approached with his knife in hand, poised to strike. The butcher sniffed the air and with a sudden roar, he spun around to swing the cleaver at Spider's head. The lithe man leant backwards, just as the heavy blade sailed passed and then darted forward, slashing Vanja's sharp edge across the butcher's throat. The blade created a neat gash across the man's jugular and a heavy stream of red flowed from the wound. The butcher roared, causing a splutter of blood to dribble from his mouth and to Spider's utter confusion, the man raised the cleaver above his head to strike again.

"In-terest-ing," commented Spider, as he dodged to one side of his seemingly inhuman opponent's blow and immediately lunged forward to stab Vanja's point in to the man's cranium. The ornate knife blade sank deep into his head and when Spider withdrew it, the man just growled. The blood-covered butcher began to violently swing the cleaver back and forth, leaving him no choice but to retreat. The captives who could stand, or had not yet lost their minds, all pleaded to be freed, as the slender man fought fearlessly against their torturer. The butcher's frenzied assault forced Spider's back against the wall and the crazed man snarled in victory as it slashed its cleaver down to kill him. Just as the heavy blade descended, Spider pulled one of the nearby captives in front of him, causing the cruel weapon to become lodged in the screaming prisoner's chest. While the growling man struggled to pull the cleaver free, Spider stabbed his knife into the huge man's head and using both hands, drove Vanja's point deep in to his skull.

The pale figure looked down at the bloody body lying at his feet and lit up a cigarette. After retrieving the keys from the dead torturers belt, he set about unshackling the captives who were begging to be freed. He casually slit the throats of the ones who were beyond saving and as the last of the emaciated prisoners moved to flee the basement,

Spider grabbed a frail looking woman by the arm, "I'm looking for two young girls, where are they?"

The woman trembled at his touch and replied, "I think the one they call 'Momma' has them in the kitchen. You should get out of here! They have probably been cooked and eaten by now." Spider scowled at the woman, pushed her to the floor in disgust and strode up the steps to find 'Momma'. Standing in the hallway of the farmhouse, he watched the captives fleeing into the night and wondered if Mr White would remain hidden, or try to help the luckless individuals. Spider reasoned that it didn't really matter, as most of them would be dead, or turn infected within a day anyway. Boldly pushing the kitchen door open, he entered the grubby room to confront a large, ugly woman. The brutish individual, who looked more like a man, was frantically pressing buttons on an automaton, while licking her lips. At the back of the room, he could see a wooden cage and within it were the two girls. He noticed that although they were gagged and bound, they appeared to be unhurt.

"You cain't be in here!" shrieked the woman. "I'm COOK'IN!"

Spider flicked the cigarette stub to the floor, looked up at her and whispered, "Momma, I pre-sume?"

"Yeah! Who're you?" responded Momma angrily.

The automaton suddenly whirred in to life. "This Chef'a'matic is now ready to cook delicious, mouth-watering humans for your enjoyment, Mistress!" Spider watched as the boxlike robot, trundled over to the cage on its tracks and moved its two long arms to grab the girls. Mounted in the machines chest was a huge oven and as it picked up the children, the machine opened its oven door emitting a cloud of steam. The girls muffled cries briefly distracted Momma and as she eagerly watched the children being prepared for cooking, Spider strode across the room towards her. When the lithe man kicked the fat woman hard in the back, she was sent crashing to the floor and he then swiftly dragged the Chef'a'matic over to its dazed mistress. Before Momma knew what was happening, the man had forced her head into the robot's burning hot oven. While holding the shrieking woman down, he watched with fascination as her head quickly blackened and then burst in to flames. The fire soon spread to engulf the rest of her body and not wanting to be wasteful, Spider carved off some cooked meat to take with him.

Mr White burst into the kitchen and when he saw what Spider was doing, he raised his rifle at him. "Stay where you are, damn ya! You're as bad as the rest of these folks!"

"Per-haps," answered Spider as he casually lit another cigarette. He then untied the two girls, who immediately ran over to the old man.

"You ain't coming with us!" declared Mr White, crossly.

"No I am not," agreed Spider, as he exhaled a cloud of smoke. "I su-ggest you go east to Shadow-vale, it is rel-ative-ly safe there."

"Okay, I'll bear that in mind," said Mr White amiably. "I don't know what your problem is, but we part ways here, okay? I don't trust ya with these kids."

"Look af-ter the chil-dren," replied Spider. As he made his way to the door he stopped by Susie and held out her teddy bear.

The young girl apprehensively took the stuffed toy, gave it a hug and timidly said, "Goodbye Mister, thank you."

Spider paused at the doorway, looked back at them all and flashed a sinister grin. "You are wel-come."

Chapter Five

"Love & Faith"

Cloaked within the darkness, he sat on his motorcycle at the far side of the causeway. Spider smiled to himself as he smoked a cigarette and watched the campervan on the bridge turn about to head back east towards the town of Shadowvale. Providing they made the journey safely, he knew their chances of survival would be significantly improved once they reached the settlement. Part of him wanted to follow them there, but his path lay in the opposite direction and ever since he had received that fateful letter at the town, he had a feeling this journey would be his last. As the tail-lights of the van disappeared in to the night, Spider found himself wondering when he would meet this 'white eyed man' the Codex had spoken of. Tossing the remains of the cigarette to the tarmac, he kick-started the bike and sped away down the road. By daybreak he was nearing the end of the 10/13 highway and running parallel to the road, to his right, was the open stretch of water which surrounded the southern expanse of City-10. Dark clouds had begun to gather in the morning sky and it seemed that this day, like many others would be held in perpetual twilight. Feeling a little weary, Spider decided to pull over by the water's edge to take a break. While he sat down on the grassy embankment to have a meal, he gazed across the watery divide, to the vast city beyond and thought back to his first days in this country.

Although Vîggo had found the flight aboard the passenger jet to be quite exhilarating, Mr Johansson, who had kindly agreed to accompany him, had spent the majority of the journey feeling quite ill. Upon arrival in Los-Demones, they checked into some hotel rooms and intended to spend a week exploring the massive, sun-drenched city. Vîggo was still learning the finer points of the English language and on several occasions was dearly thankful that his friend spoke the language fluently. As neither of them was used to the region's warm climate and they were still suffering from jet-lag, they ended up spending most of those first days sheltering from the hot sun, by the hotel's pool. Vîggo was glad Marcus had agreed to help him settle into the city, before he moved to the medical college's provided lodgings and when the day came for his old friend to leave, he promised to call Vîggo on the phone whenever he could. The huge and prestigious medical college turned out to be just as grand as his former teacher had said and although his dorm room was quite small, once he had settled in, he rarely left it other than to attend classes. Despite being younger than his classmates, Vîggo's insightful knowledge of biology greatly impressed his tutors and after only a few short months, he was made a teaching assistant. As he had clearly already mastered so much in the field of biology, his tutors let him begin a more intensive study of chemistry and medical drugs.

Teaching assistants were expected to offer help to any student who asked, but Vîggo found he preferred to avoid people as much as possible and often locked himself in his room, ignoring any knocks at his door. He had come to consider people as an unnecessary distraction and was determined to remain focused purely on his studies.

Vîggo was nearing the end of his third year at the college and was now eighteen years old. It was now late December and as usual he was studying in his dorm room, but on this evening he found the din from the frivolities outside were becoming increasingly annoying. When there was an unexpected knock at his door, he finally snapped and abruptly pulled the door open. He looked out in to the dormitory corridor at the dozens of inebriated students, who were celebrating the imminent arrival of the New Year and then at the blonde-haired girl standing in front of him. Vîggo recognised the girl as one of the first year students and glared at her questioningly.

"Happy New Year, Vîggo!" said the smiling girl as she leaned forward to kiss him. When he saw the pretty girl lean towards him, he was unsure of how to react and froze.

They shared a lingering kiss and she whispered, "You do remember me, right? I'm Louisa Loveless." Vîggo stood speechless, while vacantly staring in to her green eyes and eventually nodded.

"Can I come in?" asked the girl. Vîggo liked this young woman, but was puzzled as to why she wanted to go in his room at this late hour. Surely she wasn't proposing they had sex? Louisa snapped him back to reality. "Hey, think I lost you there for a minute. I was told by my tutor, you could help me brush up on my biology?"

Vîggo felt foolish and muttered, "Yes that is quite under-stand-able."

Louisa giggled. "Sorry, your English sounds a bit funny. Where are you from anyway?"

Vîggo sighed. "I am Swe-dish, I on-ly came to this coun-try a few years a-go."

"Well, I think your accent is kind of sexy and you're not a bad kisser either," teased the girl, as she pushed past the speechless young man to enter his dorm room. They spent the next few hours talking about their studies and later they went for a walk in the night air together. The evening ended for them the same way it had begun, with a lingering kiss.

The nearby drone of a vehicle's engine shook him back to the present and on instinct he dropped to lie flat by the grassy roadside. From the cover of the dead undergrowth, he observed as an old station wagon slowed and then came to a stop right next to his motorcycle.

As he heard the car door open and the brisk approach of footsteps, Spider craned his head to look up at the driver through the long grass. The individual was now stood next to his bike and when he caught the faint smell of gasoline on the wind, he realised the driver intended to siphon the remaining fuel from his chopper. With his mouth set in a snarl, he drew Vanja from his coat pocket and stood up to confront the thief. The nun dropped the fuel can with fright and raised her hands in surrender, while hurriedly speaking in what Spider believed to be Spanish.

"Do you speak Eng-lish?" asked the man firmly.

"Please, do not hurt us," replied the frightened woman staring at his knife. "I just take fuel".

Spider scowled at the nun and shook his head. "Not from me Sis-ter." An unexpected murmuring from the back seat of the car gained his attention and he looked at the woman quizzically, before peering inside the vehicle. Huddled on the back seat and muttering in quiet prayer, were three old nuns.

Vîggo observed the elderly women with intrigue and turned to the younger nun. "Why are they pray-ing?"

She was clearly puzzled by his question and responded, "They pray that God will forgive our sins." Spider sighed, lit a cigarette and walked back to the motorcycle.

After mounting the bike, he took the cigarette from his lips and looked to the scared woman, "You have no-thing I want. If you wish to re-main alive, keep head-ing east." The man then accelerated away down the long highway, leaving the group of nuns both relieved and confused.

The sun was low in the grey skies when he eventually reached the highway exit, which would lead him on to the long road to City-6. Due to a lack of sleep and only having recently recovered from an illness, Spider found he was in dire need of rest. After travelling another dozen miles, he arrived at the outskirts of a small town. He pulled the bike over next to a wooden sign at the roadside marked 'Welcome to Chastity'. The sign continued to creak noisily as it swung gently in the breeze and Spider squinted into the dwindling daylight to survey the streets ahead. Many of the suburban houses were lying in a state of severe disrepair from the recent event, but a grand looking church at the town's centre appeared to have been left curiously unscathed. After parking the chopper out of sight in a nearby alley, he made his way to the double doors at the front of the church.

He was unsurprised to find the entrance was locked and tentatively knocked on the heavy doors. A few seconds passed and as he started to consider looking for an alternative place to rest, a small shutter opened in the door, to reveal an elderly man with bushy eyebrows peering out.

"Hello, my son, how may I help you?" asked the priest.

"I re-quire a place to sleep." The old clergyman's face disappeared from the shutter and there was a brief delay as he released the door locks.

The priest then beckoned from the open door and once Spider had entered, the elderly man quickly closed the door behind him. "I am Father Stadler. You are welcome to eat with us and rest here, my son."

Spider eyed the man suspiciously. "Us?"

The father chuckled. "Yes. Just earlier today another family arrived on my doorstep. It is my privilege to help God's children before I send them on their journey, especially in such dark times."

"I have al-ready eat-en," he replied curtly.

"As you wish, my son, but I insist you at least greet the others, before you turn in to sleep," said the old man with a crooked smile.

Spider was very tired and dearly tempted to cut this old fool's throat just to silence him, but just spat, "Lead on Priest." Stadler led him in to a connecting hall, where three others sat waiting around a long dining table.

"I'm really hungry, is it time to eat yet?" asked the small boy, who was perhaps seven years old.

"Jimmy!" chastised the woman sat next to him. "I am sorry, Father, we are all very tired and hungry."

The old man nodded. "It's quite all right and don't worry, Jimmy, we will all eat shortly." The priest then turned to Spider, "These are the Franklins, they are the family I mentioned earlier."

Spider stared at the African American family and noticed they didn't seem to be carrying any gear or weapons. "They are un-wise to be un-armed."

The husband smiled at his wife and child, before standing up from the table to shake Spider's hand, "Hi, I'm Richard. This here is my wife, Hannah and that's my boy, Jimmy. The Father has assured us it's quite safe here."

Spider ignored the man's outstretched hand and lit a cigarette. "No-where is tru-ly safe."

The priest looked over at the smoking individual with disdain. "This is a house of God! I would ask you hand all weapons over until you depart and please do not smoke in here!"

While holding Vanja ready in his pocket, Spider exhaled smoke and simply replied, "Un-accept-able."

The flustered clergyman muttered, "Well at least extinguish your cigarette!"

Ignoring the priest's protests, the gaunt man walked back to the aisle in the main hall and settled down to sleep on a pew.

As the rising sun's rays filtered through the stained glass windows, he was abruptly awoken by the deafening chimes of the church bells. Spider swiftly arose and was perplexed to find the three members of the Franklin family lying sprawled in the aisle, between the pews. Holding his fingertips to their necks he checked them for a pulse and after a few moments he quickly came to realise they had been drugged, likely by the priest's 'free' meal. The incessant ringing bells concerned him greatly and he had a nagging suspicion why they were being sounded. He could see the main doors were open wide and moving avidly through the streets towards the church, was a shambling horde of Infected.

"A Father must tend his flock!" screamed the unseen clergyman from somewhere on a floor above. "Feast upon thy flesh and know your God loves you my children!"

Mr Franklin struggled to his feet and when he saw his family, he rushed over to check on them.

"The man's insane!" shouted Richard, trying to make himself heard over the bells, "We need to close those doors!"

Spider grimaced and shook his head as he shouted back, "Too late!" As the first of the towns many rotting inhabitants staggered through the doors, he raced to the various exits about the church in hope of escape, but found they were all firmly locked. While Mr Franklin dragged his unconscious wife and son to the rear of the chamber, Spider continued to frantically search for a way out.

Realising there was nowhere to run, he reluctantly returned to stand beside Mr Franklin, who was huddled on the floor with his family. Even though Richard was clearly terrified of the encroaching horde, in a bid to protect his helpless wife and son he had picked up a heavy looking candlestick to use as a weapon.

Spider looked down at the young boy and the child's mother. "I can give your fam-ily a quick death if you wish?"

"What?" asked the man in disbelief and looked at his family lying at his feet. "We can't do that. Do you think we can fight them?"

Spider looked up at the dozens of rotting, former people and grinned. "Per-haps, but it may prove diff-icult to pro-tect your fam-ily."

The first of the voracious walking corpses had already reached them and Spider leapt forward with Vanja in hand. As the closest Infected lunged to bite him, he used the creature's attack against it and held out Vanja's point to intercept its brain. As soon as the stinking corpse had skewered its head upon the knife, he withdrew it and kicked a second looming Infected in the torso, knocking it backwards into a few others of its wretched kind. Spider had no time to check upon Richard, but he could hear him furiously swinging his makeshift club against the tide of advancing monsters, who sought to devour his family's flesh.

Two Infected threw themselves forward to grab hold of Spider, but the agile man sprang backwards and as the creatures fell to the floor, he brought the heel of his boot stomping down to crush their skulls. Through the cacophony of rasping groans, Spider heard a cry for help and instantly knew Richard was in trouble. After kicking another of the fetid creatures in the chest, he span about to see two of the Infected had grabbed hold of Richard and without hesitation, hurled his throwing knife. The small blade pierced in to the back of an Infected's head, causing it to drop lifelessly to the floor. With only one creature now bearing down upon him, Richard managed to repel his remaining attacker and continued to defend his family from the surrounding horde. Spider brought Vanja's sharp edge across another hostile's throat to decapitate it, but once more he had to step back to avoid the grasping hands of the rotting crowd. The two men were now standing side by side, with their backs to the wall and had nowhere left to turn. Spider pulled the sawn-off shotgun from inside his coat, levelled the gun at the crowd and squeezed the trigger. There was a thundering boom as several of the foul creatures were blown to pieces, but the numerous dead continued to advance upon them.

His gaze turned from the relentless swarm of Infected to the smoking gun in his hand and he sighed. "Dis-appoint-ing."

Chapter Six

"The Blood Trail"

As the morning sun began to ascend in to the murky grey sky, the battered van pulled up outside the farmhouse. The four motley individuals had just returned from a fruitless search for food and as they disembarked the van, they noticed it was oddly quiet.

"Where the fuck is everyone?" asked the muscular Hispanic man, sounding quite perturbed.

"It is eerily silent, non?" responded the woman beside him in her soft French accent.

Drake stopped to leer at the athletic, yet voluptuous blonde. "Hey, French bitch, if you want us to make some noise, I'm good to go here," said the man gesturing to his crotch. Although Angeline had only recently turned thirty, she had experienced a lot in her life and had even served a couple of years in the military. After receiving a dishonourable discharge for drug abuse, she had tried to take an overdose, but that had just made things worse. Ever since that suicide attempt she had suffered from mood swings and had found it increasingly difficult to control her temper. Angeline ambled up to stand in front of Drake and batted her eyelashes at him. She slowly caressed her hands over her alabaster skin, from her large heaving breasts, to her taut stomach and then down between her legs.

Her vivid green eyes stared lustfully at the man and as her full pouting lips began to smile, she suddenly shrieked, *"You filthy dog!"* With a stiletto dagger in hand, she had just retrieved from a sheath on her inner thigh, Angeline leapt at the man, screaming. Before Drake could react, she had tackled him to the ground and the two of them thrashed about in the dirt. The sound of a gunshot brought their fight to a rapid halt and they both looked up at the old man holding the two revolvers, who now held one trained at each of their heads.

"The fucking bitch took my eye!" roared Drake, who was still lying in the muck and clutching his blood covered face.

"Ah, magnifique," remarked the smiling woman, as she marvelled at the man's burst eyeball on the end of her dagger and promptly stood up, while brushing the dirt from her long blonde hair.

The old man they knew as 'Carter' looked at them both with disdain as he lowered his guns, "Anymore shit like that and I'll put the two of you in the dirt for good, you hear me?" Angeline and Drake were both wary of Carter, despite his old age; the man was very proficient at killing with those pistols.

They both nodded in silence and while Drake hurried away to tend to his bleeding eye socket, Carter headed off to search around the property for any signs of their missing comrades. Angeline went to check on her little brother, who was still asleep in the van. She opened the rear doors of the vehicle and gazed upon her brother deep in slumber. Claude was twenty seven years old, stood well over six feet tall and weighed about twenty five stone. He had suffered an accident as a child, which had left him mentally retarded. Claude now possessed a mental age of an eight year old and had come to heavily rely upon his big sister to look after him for most of his life. He was highly protective of Angeline and since the event the huge man had actually protected her on several occasions. When their father had fallen gravely ill a few months ago, he had insisted that Angeline travel abroad to help run his business in America. She sorely missed her beautiful chateaux in Bordeaux and every day she seemed to feel a little more homesick. The siblings had been travelling in a subway train in City-13 when the event had occurred and they had been trapped in those lightless tunnels for nearly two weeks without food. Faced with starvation, they had eventually resorted to cannibalism and eaten the flesh of the dead passengers. They had only arrived at the farmstead ten days ago and Claude's new found insatiable appetite for human flesh worried Angeline greatly.

"Rise and shine, mon petit frère, we are at the farm," said Angeline, as she gently shook the snoring man. Claude initially looked at her with a blank expression, but when he realised who she was, he sat up and gave her an enormous grin.

"Time for dinner?" yawned Claude in his dull-toned voice, as he climbed out of the van.

"Oh, Claude, you eat too much," replied Angeline, who then kissed her brother on the cheek, making him emit a boisterous laugh. As they walked to the house, they were met by Carter and Drake coming out of the front door. The two men looked to be in a state of confusion.

"Momma and the others are dead," exclaimed Carter. "All our food downstairs is either dead, or gone walking."

"Is Pig okay? I like him," remarked Claude while smiling at the sky, quite oblivious to the events unfolding around him.

Carter shook his head. "Yeah well, the bastard's got him too, found Pig sliced up in his basement."

"Shit, didn't think anyone could kill that hombre," commented Drake, "We should find the assholes who did this and fuck 'em up!"

"I'm inclined to agree," said Carter. "There ain't much point staying here now anyhow. Angeline, you and your brother start loading up the van with any supplies left in the farmhouse."

"D'accord, but what will you be doing?" enquired Angeline, somewhat curious.

Carter gestured to the mass of footprints in the dirt leading from the front door. "Me and Drake will scout the area for tracks, the sons of bitches who left these can't have gotten far."

It was nearing nightfall by the time the two men returned to the farm and with a little help from her simple minded brother, Angeline had loaded the vehicle with the remaining useful items scavenged from the house.

Drake was holding a heavy looking duffle-bag and Angeline had no doubts regarding what it would contain, *"Superbe, you are back. You found something, non?"*

Carter gave her a nod and slapped the bulging bag on Drake's back, which she could now see was full of bloody hunks of meat, "Yeah we did. Rounded up a couple of the runaways from the basement, got us some extra food for the journey."

"Très bien, but where are we going?" asked Angeline while heaving a sigh, she dearly wished they had brought back some food which wasn't human flesh.

"Found something interesting, frenchie," said Drake glaring hatefully at her with his one seeing eye. "Found tracks from a motorcycle on the nearby hill and they turn west towards route six."

"We leave at first light, so you best go get some rest," ordered Carter. Angeline didn't care for the way Drake was staring at her, but reasoned the man wouldn't be stupid enough to attack her in front of Carter and went back inside the house. She found her brother dozing in one of the rooms and lay down on a mattress near him to get some sleep.

Claude was already half asleep, but mumbled, "Are we going somewhere?"

"Oui mon petit frère, but alas I do not know where," lamented Angeline.

"Will there be food there?" muttered the drowsy man.

"Hopefully," replied the tired woman. *"Bonne nuit, Claude."*

The sun had only just begun to rise and in the farmhouse's kitchen, Angeline was having some difficulty with her brother regarding his breakfast. She had just given him the only tin of food she could find, in a desperate bid to sway him from his constant cravings for human flesh and he was far from grateful.

"Claude, eat your breakfast," said Angeline, who herself was feeling weak from hunger.

The huge man screwed up his face in disgust as he stared at the can of beans in his hand and hurled it to the floor, bellowing, "No!"

"Claude, eat your food!" instructed his sister sternly.

"No!" shouted Claude as he stamped his foot in protest, "Want people meat!" The despairing blonde-haired woman shrieked in rage as she swept the crockery from the table, sending it all crashing to the floor and after seeing her brother's vacant expression, she slumped to the ground in defeat.

"Face the facts, lady, your brother's got the taste for it now, just like the rest of us and don't go thinking you're any different, cos you aint," said Carter, who had watched the entire scene unfold from the doorway. He turned to look at Claude, "I've got some meat for you boy, come and take a look." The simple minded man looked at his distraught sister with a measure of concern, but upon hearing the promise of the food he desired, he smacked his lips and hurriedly exited the room with Carter. The despondent Angeline didn't move from the dirty kitchen floor where she lay and once she was alone, promptly burst in to tears. Carter's words troubled her deeply, was the old man right?

Was she truly the same as Drake and Carter? She had eaten the dead to survive, but even now part of her almost wished she had died instead. Whether raw, or cooked, eating the flesh of humans still made her want to vomit and in her heart Angeline knew that would never change.

Barely an hour later, all four of them were hurtling along the highway in the van and when they spotted black smoke rising from the bottom of a steep embankment amidst some woods, Carter brought the vehicle to a screeching halt.

An overturned station wagon could be seen at the bottom of the slope and Drake looked to Carter. "One of us should check it out, could be some useful gear down there."

Carter nodded. "Go take a look, girl, and don't take all day about it."

"*Pourquoi moi?*" grumbled the woman as she departed the van.

As Angeline started to descend the stony slope, she slipped backwards and slid down to the base of the hill on her backside.

Grimacing in discomfort, she briefly paused to caress her chafed rear and then proceeded to approach the crashed car. When she crouched down to look inside the back of the overturned vehicle, Angeline was shocked to see two elderly nuns with blood smeared faces, gnawing on another old woman's body. The two Infected hissed when they saw her, but continued to bite in to the corpse, tearing off pieces of the dead woman's face to eat. A whispering voice from elsewhere in the car caused her to peer cautiously to the front of the vehicle, where she could see another nun suspended by her seat-belt. The young, Hispanic woman was uttering a prayer and shaking with fear, as she stared into the car's mirror at the gruesome spectacle behind her.

"What's taking so long, bitch?" shouted Drake from high above on the roadside. Ignoring the annoying Mexican, Angeline carefully leaned through the driver's open window to collect a box of food supplies lying just inside the door. When the trembling nun laid eyes upon her, Angeline looked up at the seat belt preventing the woman's escape and then her exposed neck. It occurred to her that with a single stoke of her dagger, she could kill, or free this poor girl, but Drake and Carter would want the nun brought back to their van. Those two men would likely rape, kill and eat this poor girl, but did she want this young woman's death on her already overburdened conscience?

Once Angeline had struggled back up the hill and climbed into the rear of the van, she showed the others the box of supplies.

Carter noticed Angeline's stiletto dagger was covered in blood and commented, "You had a little company huh?"

The woman nodded. "*Mais oui, nothing I could not handle.*"

In the wood below, the young nun watched as the van slowly drove away. She looked at the food items her rescuer had purposefully left behind and then to the three, now lifeless bodies of her former friends. The stranger on the motorcycle they had met the day before had suggested they head eastwards and after offering a final prayer for her fallen sisters, she continued in that direction along the road.

Chapter Seven

"Retribution"

Under the bright light of the morning sun, it moved with purpose through the town streets and once the large being had detected its target, it came to a stop. Changing its vision to thermal imaging, the entity analysed the target's surrounding environment. The calculated probability of the target's death was now exceeding safety parameters and this eventuality dictated the machine's orders to remain undetected were now over-ridden. Having analysed the schematics of the large building and the proximity of the hostile subjects in relation to the target, the automaton engaged one of its many weapon systems.

The encircling crowd of stinking Infected attacked relentlessly from all sides and although death now seemed inevitable, Spider fought on regardless. He stabbed his knife through one of the foul creature's skulls and using his alternate arm, repelled another by striking it in the face with his elbow. The sheer weight of the pressing horde forced the two struggling men to the ground and as the dead fell upon them to feed, there was a sudden crash of breaking glass, followed by an immediate fiery explosion. The huge stained glass windows about the hall shattered into thousands of fragments, as the blast of intense burning heat engulfed the church. The legion of walking corpses was immolated within the bright orange flames and when the smoke cleared, the church floor was left piled high with the charred bodies of the dead. Spider coughed repeatedly as he pushed his way through the piles of blackened corpses atop him and after a few moments managed to climb to his feet. Apart from the ringing in his ears and some minor burns he was largely unhurt, but whatever, or whoever had caused that timely explosion troubled him a great deal.

"Oh God, no!" wailed Richard, as he held the lifeless bodies of his wife and son in his arms. "I let them die," blurted the man, as tears streamed down his cheeks. Spider looked at the crying man cradling his dead family and remembered having felt the same, when his loved ones had died.

"They like-ly felt no pain," commented Spider as he brushed the ash from his long leather coat. He casually lit a cigarette using one of the nearby burning bodies and gave Richard a sideways glance. "If you are look-ing for some-one to blame, per-haps we should find the priest." Noticing one of the interior doors had been blown from its hinges by the explosion, he peered into the adjoining room to find a staircase leading to the floor above. After collecting his holdall and retrieving his knife Vanja from the skull of an Infected, he headed up the stairs. Richard laid his son's body gently on the floor beside his mother, kissed them both goodbye and left to find his family's killer. The upper floor consisted of a short corridor and Richard found Spider listening outside a closed door.

Spider extinguished his cigarette on a wall and gestured to the door. "He is in-side."

Just as Spider had anticipated, the man hurried past him in an incandescent rage to confront the priest. The tall figure peered through the open door and watched with interest as the two men in the next room came face to face.

"What have you done!" screamed the clergyman. "My beloved children!"

"You killed my family, you sick twisted fuck!" cried Richard, as he tackled the old man to the ground and begun to repeatedly strike him about the head with his bare fists.

The bloody and battered priest cackled as he looked up at his breathless attacker. "Barabbas, kill!" In an instant, a mass of black fur and teeth leapt at Richard from the shadows beside him. The large dog's brutal attack barrelled him across the floor and the snarling hound rushed forward to tear out his throat. While the stunned man battled to keep the ferocious beast from clamping its jaws around his jugular, Stadler staggered towards the window to seek his escape. Spider had suspected the Father would have some means of defending himself and had purposefully allowed Richard to enter the room first, to reveal whatever the old man had planned. Spider strode into the room and darted forward to thrust Vanja's sharp point into the back of the dog's skull, causing the beast to emit a sharp yelp. As the creature's heavy corpse collapsed atop Richard, he turned to face the fleeing clergyman, who was trying to climb out of the open window and deftly tossed the small throwing knife in to the priest's trailing leg.

Stadler squealed in pain. "It's not fair, why has God forsaken me!" Spider walked up behind the deranged individual and yanked the small blade free from the back of his calf, making the man whimper. The priest was now on his knees, with his upper body hanging out of the window and while holding him in that position, Spider trod a foot down hard upon the man's bleeding leg wound. The sound of Stadler's agonised screams brought a wicked grin to his gaunt face and he cast his gaze to the street below, where just beyond the churchyard's metal perimeter fence, a few of the town's surviving Infected were gathering.

"Release me, I am a man of God!" screeched Stadler. Spider smiled as he let the clergyman stand up and then promptly kicked the elderly man square in the back, sending the screaming priest plummeting from the window. He watched with satisfaction as the Father was skewered upon the metal railings below and the man's own beloved children began to rip his still twitching body apart.

Richard walked over to the window to stand beside the pale man and looked down at the grisly scene outside. "Is the bastard dead?"

Spider stared down at the remains of the bloody carcass impaled upon the fence and turned his gaze to Richard. "I am fair-ly cer-tain."

Richard was still trying to accept the grim reality that his family were now dead and muttered under his breath, "What am I meant to do now?"

He recognised the forlorn look in the man's eyes and as he moved to exit the room, Spider paused in the doorway. "You han-dle your-self quite ad-mir-ably. If you wish to, you may accom-pany me."

Richard blinked and looked at the man. "What about my family?"

"They are dead," responded Spider, nonchalantly lighting a cigarette with a metal lighter he had just retrieved from his pocket.

"Shouldn't we bury them at least?"

Spider glared at the man, while taking another drag of his cigarette. "This town is full of In-fected, we can-not re-main here." When the two men wandered down the stairs, they found the entire ground floor filled with smoke and flames. The fires from the earlier explosion had now spread throughout the church and faced with the surrounding inferno, they fled outside to the street.

When Spider began to walk away, Richard called out, "Hey, where are you going?"

Tossing the cigarette stub to the pavement, he replied, "To co-llect my motor-cycle."

"Well, my pick-up is just parked across the street," said Richard, gesturing to a nearby vehicle. "I guess you could load your bike on the back of my truck, if you want?" The stoic man nodded in agreement and walked away briskly to find the chopper. A few minutes later, they had wheeled the bike on to the rear of Richard's vehicle and were soon heading west out of Chastity. Spider was unsure of how greatly he could trust his new travelling companion, but was glad he would be able to conserve his bike's dwindling fuel supply for a while longer. After witnessing the recent explosive intervention at the church, he had little doubt the 'white eyed man' would soon make himself known to him.

From the outskirts of the town, the machine silently observed the target's departure and immediately sent a situation report to inform its masters, that the target would soon be approaching the engagement zone.

"So where you from originally?" asked Richard, trying to make conversation with his eerily quiet passenger, while driving through the bleak landscape.

"Swe-den," replied Spider, as he suddenly pulled out Vanja from his pocket.

When the driver saw the knife he almost crashed. "Fuck, man! What you doing with-" Before Richard finished his sentence, the man took out a whetstone from his black holdall and began to gently sharpen the vicious looking blade.

The man's fearful reaction caused Spider to smile and whispered, "I have no in-tention of kill-ing you, Rich-ard."

"Well, that's good news I guess," replied the man, somewhat incredulous. "You do know it's not normal to go around telling people stuff like that, right?" Spider didn't answer and continued to use the whetstone to hone Vanja's already sharp edge. They drove west along route six for several hours, often passing derelict cars and groups of Infected shambling amidst the barren wasteland. As the sun was beginning to set, Richard pulled off the highway in to a rest-stop, to get some sleep. Once they had stopped, Spider got out of the truck and headed over to inspect the few abandoned vehicles that were parked nearby. One van in particular caught his eye and as he approached the vehicle, the winds began to blow more strongly.

From the pick-up, Richard looked out with concern at the surrounding flat desolate landscape and then to the rapidly darkening sky. He observed the stranger, who had not yet told him his name, stride against the gathering tempest, towards the food wagon and decided he should go have a look around.

With his black leather coat billowing in the wind behind him, Spider stood outside the van's door, poised to enter. After collecting his knife, he hauled the door open and stepped inside the vehicle's grimy interior. He edged cautiously across the sticky floor of the 'Mr Greasey's' hotdog wagon, which was littered with sodden napkins and polystyrene food cartons. Upon hearing a creak from behind him, Spider immediately turned to face the perpetrator and acting on instinct, brought Vanja's razor edge against the terrified Richard's throat.

"Hey! It's me!" cried the startled man. "I just came to give you a hand for Christ's sake!"

He removed the knife from his neck and gave him a nod. "As you wish. You may search here, while I take a look in the cab."

Richard shrugged. "Sure, order the black guy around why don't you." Spider was mystified by the man's racial remark and went to investigate the front of the van. The van's cab reeked of urine and after a little searching he found a fuel can under the driver seat, which was nearly full.

"Hey! Can you give me a hand here?" shouted Richard, "Might be something good in here."

After placing the fuel can in his holdall, Spider returned to the rear of the wagon, to find the man heaving on the door of a large refrigeration unit.

"I think it's jammed," grumbled Richard, while continuing in his attempt to pry the metal door open. The freezer unexpectedly burst open and Richard let out a short scream, as the decaying body of a tubby hotdog vendor fell out from within.

"Mis-ter Grea-sey, I pre-sume?" whispered Spider, seemingly quite unfazed by the sudden appearance of the corpse. The bottom of the freezer was full of empty hotdog tins, but they found several unopened cans amongst the pile.

"Looks like the poor guy locked himself in there, probably to hide," commented Richard.

As Spider passed the man a few tins, he casually remarked, "He died of suff-ocation."

"Are you a Doctor or something?"

Spider seemed to ignore him and appeared to be more interested in the deceased man lying at their feet. Having noticed the hotdog vendor's eyes had begun to bleed, Spider crammed the fat cadaver back in the freezer. They walked back to the pick-up in silence and once they were both sat in the truck, Spider answered his question. "I was a surgeon and my name is Vîggo Hell-strom, but you may call me Spider."

"Spider?" queried the man. "Shit, I've heard of you! Weren't you some sort of serial killer?"

"Per-haps," responded Spider cryptically, as he opened one of the tins of hotdogs with his knife.

"Look, all I know is that you saved my life back at that church, so I say we leave the past in the past, you hear what I'm saying?"

"A-greed," replied the man, while glaring at the open tin of food in his hands with disdain.

As the two men struggled to eat the tinned food, Richard turned to Spider and held up one of the rubbery sausages. "Were these things always this bad?"

Spider grimaced. "They are ex-actly as I re-member... Aw-ful."

Chapter Eight

"Unexpected Company"

The howling winds had finally eased and under the cover of night, a skulking figure crept closer to the truck. While crouched down beside the pick-up, the old man stroked his wispy beard as he contemplated the lock under the beam of his flashlight. Upon hearing movement from inside the vehicle, he deliberated before risking a peek through the passenger window and was relieved to see the man in the driver seat was still sleeping. Swiftly returning to the task of siphoning gas from the truck, he pried the fuel flap open with a screwdriver and as he took a short length of rubber hose from his duffle-bag, he paused. Something was troubling him and when he realised what it was, he began to panic. He had observed two men sat in this vehicle when he had first arrived, where had the pale skinny man gone? The sudden presence of a cold knife edge pressed against his throat answered his question and the shock caused him to drop his belongings to the concrete.

"Bugger," mumbled the elderly thief. He screwed up his eyes, awaiting the fateful cut, which would end his life, but the stinging blade at his neck unexpectedly vanished. As he began to question what was happening, he received a heavy blow to the top of his balding head, rendering him unconscious.

The groaning individual awoke with a start, to find himself in a confined dark space, with his hands tied behind his back.

When Spider heard the muffled cries for help, he opened the trunk of the car and shone the man's own flashlight upon him. "Hell-o. Did you en-joy your rest?"

The elderly man looked up at him with pleading eyes. "Look, I'm sorry I tried to steal your gas, okay? Please just let me go!"

"I am in a gen-erous mood, so I will give you a litt-le time to con-vince me of your use-fulness," replied Spider, as he pulled the struggling Infected in front of him. "At the mo-ment, Mis-ter Greas-ey here is gagged and bound, but I do not know how long he will re-main so." Before the old man could argue, Spider pushed the rotting hotdog vendor into the trunk next to him and slammed the lid shut. While sat on the rear of the vehicle, Spider lit a cigarette, and as he listened to the screams of the thrashing occupants within, he smiled.

The thief could barely hear himself scream over the rasping of the hungry Infected and shouted, "Please let me out! I can give you something you want!" Spider slid off the car to the ground and after taking a minute to finish his cigarette, he pulled open the violently shuddering trunk.

He looked down at his petrified captive and the growling Infected, which had almost bitten through the thick gag about its face.

"Ex-plain what it is, that you pre-sume I want," stated Spider coldly.

The trembling man could barely meet the gaze of this captor's dark ringed eyes, but blurted, "In my car, there are materials! I'm an engineer!"

Intrigued by his words, Spider hauled the emaciated man from the trunk, threw him down to the tarmac and closed the lid. While standing with a foot on the wheezing man's chest, he stared down at him and asked, "What is your name?"

The old man began to cough and nervously responded, "Clarence."

Spider grinned. "Well Cla-rence, what are these mat-erials you men-tioned?"

"I got some layers of Kevlar-weave, maybe I could armour your coat for you?" spluttered the man, while still trying to catch his breath. "I'm retired now, but I used to work for the military and I kinda kept a few things when I left... you know how it is."

"You are clear-ly a thief, but I will give you un-til sun-rise," said Spider, as he pulled the man to his feet and untied his hands. "If I am dis-appoint-ed by your work, you will be re-turning to your ve-hicle's trunk, under-stand?" The man gulped at the grim prospect and nodded, as Spider handed him his long leather coat. After rushing to his car, the flustered Clarence began to rummage through his bags, to find the necessary tools and materials.

As the first rays of sunlight shone over the horizon, Richard awoke in his pick-up, to find his blond-haired companion sat bare-chested on the hood of his truck. He wound down the window and shouted, "What the hell man? You're gonna freeze your ass off!" Richard took a swig of water from his thermos flask and once he had exited his truck, offered some to Spider, who he now realised, was observing an old man in a nearby car.

"Who's the old guy?" asked Richard uneasily.

Spider accepted the flask and took several sips, before passing it back. "That is my good friend Cla-rence. He has kind-ly off-ered to fix my coat."

Richard raised an eyebrow in disbelief and as he walked away, mumbled, "Yeah right, whatever man."

"The sun has now ris-en," announced Spider as he approached the open door of the car, where Clarence was frantically working to complete his task.

"It's finished!" replied Clarence, holding up the coat. "I did a pretty good job too, even if I do say so myself."

Spider eyed the garment suspiciously. "It looks the same."

The old man smiled anxiously. "Well, that's the idea. The interior of this article of clothing now has a Kevlar-weave lining. Apart from the small increase in weight, no-one should be able to tell the difference."

Spider put on the familiar garment and instantly felt the added weight. "Time for a litt-le test per-haps?" He held the open coat away from his body with one hand and viciously stabbed Vanja's sharp tip into the taut leather, but to his surprise the knife barely nicked the surface of the material. "Most im-pressive," remarked Spider.

"So I won't have to visit Mister Greasey again?" asked Clarence apprehensively.

Spider beamed a sinister grin. "You are a talen-ted in-dividual, you should tra-vel with us."

Now that his car was out of fuel, Clarence knew he wouldn't survive walking the road alone and grudgingly answered, "That would be very helpful, what did you say your name was?"

"You may call me Spi-der," replied the slender figure as he buttoned his coat.

The three men spent the next few hours travelling along the open highway in an awkward silence and as the pick-up climbed over the crest of a hill, City-6 came in to view. Richard brought the truck to a sudden halt and they all stared in disbelief at the devastation before them. From what they could see, it seemed the entire city had been levelled to rubble and was now shrouded by a greenish smog.

Richard sighed. "Time to turn back I guess, that shit looks nasty."

"Could be radioactive," commented Clarence, who was sat between the others.

"We wait," responded Spider quietly.

"Wait?" retorted Richard sarcastically. "Wait for what? Christmas?"

"No," replied Spider, as he stared ahead into the murky cloudbanks. "Him." While the other two men squinted into the cloud with confusion, Spider got out of the truck and ventured through the smog.

"That dude is damn crazy," whispered Richard as he watched the man disappear from sight.

Clarence looked at him and smiled. "You know, we could just leave him."

Richard frowned. "What sort of asshole do you take me for? Look, the guy may be crazy, but he saved my life."

Clarence gestured at the dense fog. "So are you going in after him then?"

"Probably best if we wait here, I'm sure he'll be back in a minute." Clarence gave him a doubting look, but said nothing.

Spider continued to move blindly through the surrounding mists, to approach the shadowy form standing in the road ahead. As he drew closer, he could now see the mysterious figure was a middle aged man, dressed in a smart suit and upon closer inspection, he noticed the pupils of the man's eyes were oddly white in colour.

"Good afternoon, Mister Hellstrom, I have been expecting you. My name is Mister Gaunt," said the man in a distinguished British accent. "I trust your journey was not too arduous?"

Spider snarled at the man, "You sent me a picture of my dead wife, what is it that you want?"

"What I want is irrelevant, Mister Hellstrom," responded the man calmly. "However, our employers at Sheltercorp wish for you to be reunited with your very much 'alive' spouse."

"I no long-er work for Shelter-corp. This is non-sense, I saw her die."

"I assure you, she is alive and if you wish to see her again, you will need to travel through City-6, to reach the town of Red-hill. Once there, you will need to attend this address," said the man as he offered him a piece of paper.

Spider snatched the note from his hand and placed it in his pocket. "I was told to tra-vel to the city of Los-Demones, not some town."

"Very true," replied Mr Gaunt. "But I was told it was of the most vital importance that you attend your appointment at that address, before continuing your journey to Los-Demones, I am dreadfully sorry I cannot be of more assistance regarding the matter." Spider was sorely tempted to torture this strangely off-putting man for some answers, but having previously worked for Shelter-corp himself, he doubted the man would have been told anything of value.

Mr Gaunt placed his briefcase on the tarmac in front of him, "To show good willing, your 'former' employers have provided you and your new found companions, with something to assist in your trek through the somewhat toxic environment of City-6. I suggest you utilise the cities rail tunnels to reach the town, as the road ahead is highly irradiated. I must go now, as I have considerable work to do." As the man walked away into the smog, he shouted back, "Goodbye, Mister Hellstrom, we shall talk again when you reach the town of Red-hill."

Richard looked on with puzzlement, as the scruffy old man seated next to him, donned a hazardous materials suit he had just retrieved from one of his bags. "What the hell you doing?"

Clarence sneered. "You can get irradiated if you want, but I'm not."

When Richard saw Spider emerging from within the fog, he left the vehicle to see what the man had discovered. "You all right?"

"I may have found some-thing of inter-est," replied Spider, as he set down the newly acquired case, to see what it contained. Upon seeing there were three gas-masks within, he equipped one and passed another to his companion. "I will be go-ing through the ci-ty to reach the town of Red-hill."

"Why can't we just take the truck along the highway?" asked the dark skinned man, as he put on the breathing apparatus.

"I have been told the road ahead is un-travers-able." An engine suddenly roared into life behind them and they looked on helplessly as Clarence drove away, into the dense mists.

"I don't fucking believe it! The asshole took my truck!" Richard shouted angrily.

"Al-so my motor-cycle," responded Spider dourly, "The man will be un-likely to make it to the town a-live, but if he should, we may be able to re-cover our ve-hicles."

Richard walked over to where the pick-up had been parked. "It looks like the jerk chucked our bags out before he left, that's something, I guess."

Spider slung his black holdall over his shoulder and began to walk towards the ruins of city-6.

"Hey, wait up!" said Richard, as he chased after him.

Chapter Nine

"Path Of Destruction"

It was starting to get dark when the battered van cruised in to the town of Chastity. A fierce wind had begun to blow and clouds of ash filled the air, diminishing the visibility of the road ahead.

"You best pull over here, Drake," said Carter. "Angeline, I want you and your brother to find us a secure place to sleep. While you're taking care of that, me and Drake will go check the local cars for any gas."

"D'accord, but where should we look?" asked the woman, while peering out the window at the dozens of surrounding houses, which all seemed to have sustained heavy damage.

"Use your damn head girl," replied Carter sternly. "And don't go taking too long about it, we ain't got much daylight left."

"Come on, mon petit frère," sighed Angeline, as she disembarked the van.

"Where we going?" yawned Claude, who hadn't been paying attention to the conversation. His sister didn't reply however, as she had just laid eyes upon the cause of the airborne ash. She watched with sadness as the intense flames burned away the last of the wooden structure's interior and the church's roof suddenly collapsed, causing a shower of red hot cinders to be cast in to the smoky air.

"Who could have done such a terrible thing?" lamented Angeline.

As Carter returned from the churchyard across the street, he commented, "Looks like our 'friends' from the farm have been busy."

Drake guffawed. "Yeah, we found the remains of a priest too. Looks like the guy was thrown on to the railings, pretty fucking nasty way to die!"

Angeline considered herself to be a Christian and was truly appalled by what had transpired here, perhaps Carter was right to have them hunt down these barbaric killers.

"Hey, girl! Quit dawdling and find us a damn place to rest up," snapped Carter irritably. Angeline cursed at him in French under her breath as she led her brother away to investigate the town houses. After looking down a few streets, mostly consisting of collapsed buildings, they came across a house which appeared to be relatively undamaged. As they moved to the front door to take a look inside, Angeline paused and glanced over her shoulder at Claude.

She was disturbed to see her brother was armed with a crude looking meat cleaver he had presumably taken from Momma's kitchen. *"Now, Claude, if we should find any survivors we give them a chance to run, comprendez-vous?"*

Claude was clearly puzzled by his sister's words. "But Carter told me—"

Angeline immediately interrupted him. *"I do not care what that imbécile said! I am your sister and I know what is best for you, Claude!"*

The large man pouted and appeared to sulk, as he followed after her into the gloomy interior of the house. The lower floor of the building appeared to have sustained heavy flood damage, leaving the walls covered in grime and mould. The pair crept cautiously up the creaking wooden staircase and she was a little relieved to see the upper floor had been left largely unscathed by the water damage. They were surprised to find a frail looking lady sat in the hallway, at the top of the stairs. Angeline quickly realised the woman must have survived by drinking the dirty looking water from a bathtub in the nearby bathroom, but was confused by the heaps of empty food wrappers lying strewn around the emaciated individual.

The woman looked up at them with bleary bloodshot eyes and whispered, "Hungry… so hungry."

Claude turned to his sister and blurted, "Yeah, I'm hungry too, can we eat her?"

Before Angeline could respond to her brother's appalling question, the skinny woman before them shrieked and fled into the bathroom. Upon hearing the sound of the door being locked, Claude beamed a wide smile as he began to slam his huge body against the obstacle in a bid to smash it open.

"Claude, stop!" shouted Angeline, as she moved to stand in his way, but the dim-witted man wasn't listening and shoved her aside to continue his assault on the door. She

knew that once her brother got an idea in his head, he generally couldn't be swayed from it and hurriedly looked about the hallway for an alternate solution. Upon spying an open window in a bedroom at the end of the corridor, she rushed over to inspect it. After climbing out on to the ledge, she began to sidestep around the exterior of the building in an attempt to reach the panicked woman, while all the time doing her utmost not to look down. Angeline just hoped she would arrive in time to stop Claude from doing something terrible. Just as she reached the open bathroom window, Claude came smashing through the wooden door.

Both the siblings were alarmed by what they saw in front of them, the frail woman was convulsing and thrashing about on the bathroom floor in a pool of blackish blood.

As the woman's already desiccated skin began to shrivel and rot, they heard the distinct sound of cracking bones emanate from within her body.

The emaciated being suddenly rose to a crouched position and hissed as it plunged its long bony fingers into Claude's rotund belly. The terrified Angeline frantically scrabbled to climb through the window, while constantly staring at the disgusting Infected burying its fingers into her brother's innards. Claude was seemingly paralysed by the intense pain and continuously howled in agony, as revolting sucking noises sounded from within his guts. She almost vomited when she realised the Infected was somehow feeding on Claude's body through its hands and leapt at the abhorrent creature with her stiletto dagger. Sensing the attack, the Infected abruptly withdrew its hands from his body, causing Claude to collapse to the timber flooring. It let out a loud hiss and scurried away before the woman could even strike. Angeline turned to face the foul being and as it dashed forward to feed once more upon her groaning brother, she lashed out with her blade. She managed to inflict a cut to its face, causing the 'Feeder' to initially recoil, but it then screeched and leapt at the woman, knocking her on to her back. The fall had winded her and she watched helplessly as the rotting Infected eagerly climbed atop her, to plunge its long bony fingers into her smooth flesh of her stomach. There was an audible crunch as Claude brought his heavy cleaver arcing down to embed in the Feeder's head. While clutching the gaping wounds in his belly with one hand, he yanked the crude blade free from the lifeless Infected's head, letting the creature's corpse drop to the floor with a dull thud.

"Sister, I don't feel well," said Claude while frowning and promptly joined the body of the Infected at his feet. When Carter and Drake returned about an hour later, they found Angeline doing her best to bandage the unconscious Claude's abdominal injuries with torn up bed sheets. As she expected, neither of the men asked any questions, or offered any aid, despite the fact Claude had now developed a fever. The others soon settled down to get some rest, but Angeline was too worried about her brother to sleep and spent the night watching over him.

At daybreak they continued their journey in the van, west along the highway and when they neared the dense mist enveloping City-6, they pulled over.

While the other two men scouted the local area for any tracks, Angeline helped her pallid looking brother out of the vehicle and passed him the last of their drinking water. *"Drink this, Claude."*

Her brother gulped down the liquid and belched. "More?"

"Non, sadly that is all we have, but I am sure we will find more soon." In truth she had no idea where they could gather more food or water. She found herself wondering if the others would attempt to kill and eat her if a solution didn't soon present itself.

"Hey, over here. I've found something!" shouted Drake. The four of them gathered around an empty metal briefcase, which had been oddly left in the middle of the road.

Carter squinted into the greenish smog, "Well, that pretty much confirms it. I doubt our killers from the farm would be dumb enough to drive through this cloud and I found two sets of fresh footprints headed for the city. Looks like we go in on foot from here."

Angeline glanced from Carter to her sickly brother who was drenched in sweat and could barely stand, *"D'accord, perhaps I should take my brother back to the town, he needs medical attention and—"*

Upon hearing this, Carter gave Drake a nod.

The Hispanic man punched her hard in the face, nearly knocking her off her feet. "You aint going nowhere, you dumb bitch!"

Carter smirked. "Look, you French whore, well or not, we stick together. We are gonna find these sons of bitches and make 'em pay for what they've done." The grey-haired man levelled one of his pistols at her. "Now I reckon you and your beloved bro should lead the way."

Angeline wiped away the stream of blood from under her nose, while glaring hatefully at the two men. She took her feverish sibling's hand and reluctantly began to cross the misty fields towards the ruins of City-6. The woman looked back at Carter and Drake who were following at a short distance behind them. She knew now it would only be a matter of time before the only use they had left for her, was as food.

Chapter Ten

"In The Mist"

Towering mounds of concrete and twisted metal lay all about the two men, as they ventured further into the smog-filled ruins of the once picturesque city.

"Wait up, dude!" shouted Richard while gasping for breath, "Look, I need to take five. Say, where we heading anyway?"

Spider looked back to observe the wheezing man, who was now leaning against a buckled mailbox and fiddling with his gas-mask. "Re-moving the mask may prove to be un-wise."

"Yeah, I know. It's just so damn itchy," replied the weary man whilst scratching his neck. "Hey, do you actually know where we're going?"

His gaunt companion gave him a blank look. "We are look-ing for some rail tu-nnels to take us south-west out of the ci-ty."

"That'll be a 'no' then," answered Richard, sounding quite unnerved. "Have you noticed how quiet this place is?"

Spider looked up at the darkening cloudy sky. "I ima-gine we may have com-pany soon e-nough. We should find shel-ter."

After travelling through a few more demolished city blocks, they came across a partially standing apartment building, and upon reaching the lobby entrance, Spider unexpectedly held up a hand signalling for his companion to wait.

"What's wrong now?" whispered Richard whilst apprehensively peering through the door's small glass window.

Spider frowned at the man's foolishness. "You would be wise to arm your-self."

"Shit, you're right," remarked the dark skinned man and began to look about the vicinity for something of use. After a minute of diligent searching, he found a metal scaffolding pole and promptly returned to the lobby doorway. Spider cast a disapproving glance at the man's inelegant weapon, before gently pushing the door open and quietly slipping inside. Richard did his best to tread lightly as he followed the slender figure into the building's lightless hallway and once they were inside they found the stairwell to the floor above was blocked by tons of rubble. Only the dust filled lobby itself appeared to be habitable and after Richard had jammed the door shut with the metal pole, they settled down in a dark corner to get some rest.

"I still can't believe they're gone," whispered Richard sombrely whilst staring down at a crumpled photograph in his dirty hands. When his companion didn't reply, he snapped, "Huh, I guess a heartless asshole like you has never had to deal with the pain that comes with the death of a loved one."

The remark caused Spider to recall several painful memories and on reaction he found himself gripping the handle of his knife. In that moment he wanted to plunge the blade through the man's heart, but instead merely blinked. "Love is weak-ness. It can cause im-mense pain. I for-got that le-sson once..."

Spider's voice trailed off as if he had drifted off into deep thought and although Richard was puzzled by his response, he decided against asking the sinister individual to explain what he had meant.

Weary and tired, Spider found himself thinking back to the earlier years of his life and the events that had led up to his new grim existence.

He and Louisa had become inseparable during their time at the medical college and upon graduating, they had moved in to a city apartment together. Vîggo had worked as a surgeon at the Los Demones general hospital for two years, but his considerable skills had recently gained him a lucrative job position at a private clinic. Life was going well for the two of them and they had even set a date to be married. Although his old tutor, Mr Johansson had now retired, he remained in regular contact via phone and was delighted to hear of Vîggo's engagement.

It was a bright summer morning and a warm breeze was blowing through the open bedroom window, causing the white lace curtains to billow in to the room. The blonde-haired couple lay naked on the bed entwined in each other's arms. Neither of them had to work this day and Louisa let out a giggle as her fiancé kissed her neck. "We can't stay in bed all day, we've got things to do!"

"Oh def-initely," replied Vîggo with a smile, as he continued to kiss down her chest.

Louisa let him continue for a minute before laughing and playfully pushing him away. "No, love, I mean it, we have things to do!"

"Rea-lly?" remarked Vîggo raising an eyebrow, as they both sat up on the bed.

She cupped her hands about his chiselled jaw and smiled. "We need to go shopping for some things."

"Shopp-ing?" enquired the man in disbelief, while gazing into her vivid green eyes.

She hesitated before calmly whispering, "I'm two months pregnant and the doctors say I'm carrying twins."

Vîggo was initially stunned, but suddenly grinned. "This is won-der-ful, but we are going to need a big-ger place to live!"

"Trust you to be all practical about this, perhaps we should buy one of those new mansions they're constructing on the north side of the river," teased Louisa.

"Good idea," answered Vîggo with a knowing grin and leant into kiss his speechless lover. As a cool breeze washed over them, they fell back to the soft bed locked in a passionate embrace.

Spider's thoughts slipped from the beautiful Louisa to the reality of the cold lobby floor, where he lay in the darkness. A few hours had likely passed since they had settled down to sleep and the metal pipe jammed in the entrance was rattling loudly. They were both now wide awake and approached the door with trepidation.

A partially illuminated face pressed up against the small window. "Lemme in! The Skulls are gonna eats me!"

Richard turned to Spider with an imploring look. "We gotta open the door, we can't just let him die!"

Spider scowled at the grubby man on the other side of the glass and gestured at the metal bar. "As you wish." Richard pulled the pole free and the old man immediately bustled through the open doorway pushing a shopping trolley filled with junk in front of him.

Richard took a few moments to look outside before once more securing the door and then turned to address the scrawny newcomer. "I saw several weird shapes moving out there, what's following you old man?"

The man stank of stale sweat and was showing a toothless grin. "Skulls!" shrieked the madman and quickly donned a tinfoil hat from his pocket whilst rolling his eyes. "There, now the nuked bastards can't hear me!" screeched the man, who then proceeded to squeal and make high pitch noises before yelling, "Making contact with the mother-ship!"

It became quickly apparent that the crazy man's wailing would alert the several creatures lurking outside to their presence and Richard noticed his pragmatic companion reaching for his knife, presumably to permanently silence the lunatic.

Just as Spider was about to bring Vanja's edge across the troublesome individual's throat, Richard hit the noisy man over the head with a tin of hotdogs. Even as the crazy man slumped to the floor, he feebly continued to make 'radio' noises and Richard was forced to strike him again, before he finally fell quiet.

"What the fuck, man!" cried Richard as his companion suddenly tackled him to the floor and forcibly held a gloved hand over his mouth. Spider raised a finger to his lips to stress the need for quiet and then pointed the same finger to the door. The first rays of daylight were filtering over the ravaged city and the silhouetted visage of a hideous fleshless face pressed to the other side of the glass caused Richard to jump. The milky-eyed creature peered through the window for a few seconds and scraped its bony fingers against the glass, before finally ambling away.

As Spider removed his hand from his mouth, Richard let out a gasp. "What the hell was that thing?"

The pale man helped him back to his feet and then lit a cigarette. "That would be one of the 'Skulls' our stin-ky friend men-tioned. I heard a ru-mour that this ci-ty was hit by mal-function-ing nu-clear wea-ponry from a near-by mil-itary base, per-haps these are the sur-vivors."

"Are we being irradiated?" asked Richard wide eyed with concern.

Spider shrugged. "Poss-ibly. Best we don't lin-ger."

Richard cautiously moved to the door and looked out at the gloomy surroundings. "Hey, I think they're leaving. I guess they don't like the sunlight."

"I suggest we leave at once, we can eat and drink on the move," said Spider as he slung his holdall over his shoulder.

"What about the stinky dude?" asked Richard looking at the old man lying at his feet. Spider just shook his head and sprinted out of the door.

"Sorry, stinky," said Richard as he moved to follow his companion, but stopped to close the door before running on. He figured it may give the old guy a fighting chance of survival against the Skulls who were likely still lurking nearby.

When the old man awoke a few minutes later, he held his aching head and groaned. He wasn't really sure what had just happened, but was pleased to find his precious collection in his trolley hadn't been stolen. The old man chuckled happily to himself; clearly his special tinfoil hat had once more repelled the hungry Skulls. Life was still worth living.

Chapter Eleven

"Turning Point"

The greenish smog hung heavy about the four figures in the dwindling daylight. The toxic air caused tears to stream down Angeline's cheeks as she struggled to draw each new breath. Her throat was raw from both breathing the poisonous smog and coughing on its acrid vapours. She looked back to her sickly brother, who faltered with nearly every step and squeezed his hand, whilst giving him a brief smile. However, the fever-stricken man barely noticed and just stared vacantly in to the mists whilst mouthing unintelligible words.

"Stay with me, Claude," whispered the woman worriedly, as she mopped his sweating brow with a handkerchief.

Drake shoved her in the back with the muzzle of his rifle and sneered, "Hola, bitch! Carter says you need to find us some fucking shelter pronto, or he's gonna cut those skanky tits off!" She shot him a withering look and fought hard to not lash out at the well-armed man.

Carter sat down on a fire hydrant in front of her. "I reckon yer retard's fucked. I suggest you get a move on before you join him."

"Non, he stays with me," replied Angeline sternly and began to lead her disorientated brother away by the hand.

Carter called after her from the darkness, "You better find us a place to hold up, girl, or you best not come back at all!"

"Great!" laughed Drake. "We'll hunt you down, bitch, and I doubt you get far with your half-dead bro!"

Angeline was in two minds. Even if she found a safe place to rest amongst all this devastation, would she return to those abhorrent men? As a group they still hadn't found any food or water supplies and that only spurred on her concerns that they would soon carve her up for food. The heavily perspiring Claude was barely coherent now and kept stopping to lean against various objects along their path. Realising the others would just leave him for dead if they went back, she began a more frantic search for somewhere for them to sleep. As the siblings traipsed through the city, it seemed every building as far as they could see had been reduced to nothing but piles of debris. Every few paces they took, her brother stopped and pushed away her hand. Eventually Claude just sat down and refused to move, obstinately shouting "NO!"

Angeline dearly wanted to scream at him to keep moving, but she knew there was little point.

The man's legs had been buckling under his own weight for some time and judging by his laboured breathing, he was now too weak to even move. She could see the wounds to her brother's belly were still weeping blood and the grim stench of decay hung about him. *"Wait here, Claude, I will be back soon,"* whispered Angeline as she bent down to kiss him on the forehead. He just gave her a baffled look and looked past her to the cloudy night sky. Leaving him alone in this awful desolate place was the last thing she wanted, but she had no choice. Knowing Carter and Drake could arrive at any moment, she dashed off into the darkness in the dwindling hope of finding a refuge for the night. Running almost blind through the maze of concrete mountains and vehicle wrecks, Angeline's body received several vicious cuts, but she continued to push on through her unforgiving surroundings. When she heard a gunshot ring out, accompanied by familiar laughter, she froze.

"Yer time's up, whore!" yelled Carter. "We got your retard up here. You wanna say goodbye before we slit his throat? You ain't got nowhere to run, missy."

Angeline had no doubt they wouldn't hesitate to kill her too, but she couldn't bring herself to leave her baby brother at the mercy of those heartless men. If they were going to die, Claude should at least have his big sister by his side. They were waiting atop the mound of debris, where she had left Claude. She was relieved to see her brother was still alive for the moment, but was alarmed to see small amounts of blood were trickling from his eyes.

"Say yer farewells quick, girlie, and then we end this," said Carter while showing a devilish grin.

Angeline glanced at the two men holding their guns at the ready and with quiet resignation knelt down beside her shivering sibling. She cradled the bewildered man's head to her chest and whispered, *"It is time for us to go to sleep now, mon petit frère."* As she released him from her embrace, Claude looked up at the tears running down his sister's cheeks with confusion and gently reached out a hand to touch her face.

"We are going to see Mother and Father again," said the woman in a hushed voice, whilst fighting back more tears welling in her green eyes.

Carter looked to Drake, who was standing over the siblings with his rifle. "Do it."

Drake cocked the gun, while leering at the woman's partially exposed chest. "Hey, frenchie, maybe after I have some fun with your body!"

Angeline closed her eyes and hugged her brother, awaiting the inevitable. Claude stared up at the grinning Drake and then to the gun he was aiming at his sister's head.

Claude's eyes grew wide with rage and bellowed, "NO!" He suddenly rose to his feet and immediately dived at the Hispanic man, forcing his hands tightly around Drake's throat.

"What the fuck?" muttered Carter in disbelief and quickly raised one of his pistols to shoot the enraged Claude, but instead found the shrieking Angeline tackling him to the ground. Whilst atop Carter, she desperately tried to hold back the old man's gun wielding hands, but when he brought up a knee to slam in to her stomach, she was sent rolling away to the concrete. They both scrambled to gain their footing and as Angeline went to draw her dagger, Carter unexpectedly hurled a brick in her direction. The crude projectile struck her hard across the temple and she was sent tumbling backwards, down the steep embankment in to the pitch black.

Was she dead? There was no light here and the fact she couldn't seem to move worried her greatly. She was freezing cold and the only warmth she could feel was from the blood flowing from the stinging gash on her head. How long had she been here? Had Claude been killed? She was so hungry and thirsty she could barely think. After lying there for some time, her eyes began to adjust to the dense gloom. From what she could see, she appeared to be on the floor of a narrow winding gulley and as she strained her eyes to familiarise herself with her surroundings, something caught her attention.

Tucked away amidst the heaps of rocks and dead upturned roots beside her, was a peculiar pale mass. With nothing to lose, she stretched out an arm to reach it and found her fingertips brushing against soft velvety fur. After a few more moments, Angeline came to realise she was caressing the lifeless shapes of several tiny canines. Although initially saddened by the apparently stillborn litter, a troubling thought occurred to her. Where were the parents? As if answering her unspoken question, a guttural growling sounded from further down the valley. She could make out the menacing shape of a huge pale-furred wolf creature slowly advancing towards her.

Angeline recalled Carter mentioning how he had encountered giant flesh-hungry wolves during his travels. The old man had referred to them as 'Howlers' and had explained how they usually hunted in packs. The mother

Howler moved directly to her silent pups and nuzzled them gently, before turning its gaze upon the prone woman beside its young. Had the woman not been so afraid, she probably would have considered the beast quite beautiful and not unlike an enormous blue-eyed Husky. Angeline couldn't help but stare at the creature's large jaws, filled with sharp teeth and when the creature suddenly darted forward, she went rigid with fright. The woman barely dared to breathe as the Howler took hold of the back of her jacket and carried her over to her young.

Before she knew what was happening, the mother was washing her head wound and had curled up around her. Despite the fact she was now a lot warmer, Angeline was still terribly confused and fearful. Did this creature truly think she was one of its young, or was it merely saving her to devour later? As fatigue once more took hold of the exhausted woman, her worried thoughts began to fade and she fell in to a deep sleep.

It had rained heavily during the night and the downpour had left the dawn skies relatively clear of the poisonous mists which usually enveloped the city. As droplets fell from the dense wreckage above, they caught the bright morning light, shining in an array of sparkling colours. Angeline watched from the muddy ground where she lay, as each new bead of water landed upon the deep puddle beside her, causing circles to ripple across its murky surface. The mother Howler had not long finished drinking from the pool and had now bounded away down the narrow valley, which consisted of the piled remnants of several once grand buildings. She tried to get up and upon finding herself too weak to stand, crawled over to the water's edge on her belly. The liquid was quite cloudy, but her thirst far exceeded her concerns and cupping her hands together, she soon had drunk her fill. Knowing she would be unlikely to find another source of palatable water anytime soon, she recovered the empty bottles from within the rucksack on her back and filled several for the days ahead. Feeling somewhat refreshed, she decided to take the opportunity to look about the floor of the secluded den and was not particularly surprised to see a plethora of human bones dotted about the area. Angeline was still unsure as to why the beast had looked after her; she could only presume the creature's maternal instincts had overridden its natural desire to feed. She wondered if the beast would continue to perceive her as one of her young, or whether perhaps it would soon come to realise its mistake and devour her like the others lying about the den. With a concerted effort she managed to stand and then proceeded to slowly amble over to the largest cluster of bones. Amongst the clutter of human remains were several scraps of clothing and after a thorough search, she was pleased to find a ration bar concealed within a shredded coat pocket. She sat back down and quickly consumed the bland tasting food, whilst trying not to think about the skeletal remains strewn all around her. Angeline was so caught up in her thoughts she hadn't noticed the Howler's return and when the pale-furred beast approached her, she let out a short shriek. Thankfully the huge wolf seemed to think the woman was playing and the blue eyed beast let out a gruff yelp of its own, before falling flat to the ground, ready to pounce. She couldn't help but laugh at the enormous creature's antics, seeing such a dangerous animal acting more like a house pet was quite bizarre.

"Ah, tres bien!" giggled Angeline nervously as the Howler dived at her, only to veer away at the last second.

It then rolled over in the dirt and once more let out a little howl, as it lay down with its massive paws stretched out in front of it. She was certain that had the beast actually collided with her, its sheer size alone would have left her badly injured. Angeline took a moment to study her furry companion, the animal was almost as large as a tow-truck and its head was probably larger than that of a bear. She noticed the Howler was still lying on its belly and watching her with apparently equal interest. The beast hadn't reacted badly to her unintentional outburst and she was now wondering if it would accept her getting up to leave. While studying the animal for any signs of animosity, she eased herself up to a crouched position and slowly rose to stand. The Howler continued to eye her up with quizzical intrigue, but remained still as the woman cautiously began to approach it.

What am I doing? She thought to herself, this is crazy, what if it attacks? She was now merely inches from the massive creature and her hand was shaking as she tentatively reached out to stroke the animal's thick white coat. Its fur felt quite coarse to the touch and when the giant wolf unexpectedly moved its head, Angeline withdrew her hand. However, the Howler just yawned, showing all of its big yellow pointed teeth and proceeded to watch her with puzzlement.

"Please, don't eat me," implored the woman hopefully, as she replaced her hand to the animal's head. She ruffled the fur between its ears and to her astonishment the beast let out another playful yelp. As much as she wanted to take this beautiful animal with her, she knew there was no way it could work out. After all, how could she look after such a creature? And what if it turned on her? Angeline moved to leave, but couldn't resist giving the placid Howler a hug before she walked away. The beast whined as it followed her down to the narrow valley's entrance and as Angeline climbed up the steep hill of broken concrete, the beast let out a single woeful howl, before wandering slowly back to its den.

Upon reaching the summit, she came to recognise the area as the hill from where she had fallen the night before. Angeline began to hurriedly search around for any signs of her brother amongst the rubble. When a faint cry on the wind caught her ear, she began to rush back and forth along the hilltop frantically searching for the source.

"Angeline!" moaned a hoarse voice from somewhere above. The woman squinted into the rising sun, to the twisted metal wreckage on the ridge above her. Without a moment's hesitation she sprinted up the embankment towards the silhouetted body apparently tethered to the remains of a neon sign. The grim sight of her naked brother ensnared by reels of bloody barbed wire was too much for her to bear and she promptly burst in to tears.

Vermin had gnawed away the lower portions of his legs and even now gulls were plucking strips of flesh from his shrieking face. His eyes had been clearly cut out with a knife and carved on his forehead were the words 'Fuck you bitch'.

"Angeline!" spluttered Claude, spraying another flood of blood from his mouth. Each breath he took forced the barbed wire across his chest and belly to cut deeper, allowing his innards to push further through the ragged tears.

"I-I am here, Claude," stammered Angeline in a hushed voice.

"I CAN'T SEE YOU!" yelled the distraught man.

Tears cascaded down her face as she placed a hand on his shredded cheek, "It will all be over soon, little brother."

"IT HURTS!" bawled Claude, while shaking with fear. "Make it go away!"

Angeline leant in close and kissed him on the forehead and whispered, "I love you, Claude."

Upon hearing his sister's familiar words, the simple man managed to smile and in that instant his sister drove her stiletto dagger up through his jaw, into his brain. Bathed in the morning light, the forlorn woman collapsed beneath her brother's still body, sobbing broken-heartedly into the dust.

Chapter Twelve

"Parting Ways"

Amongst the grey expanse of the destroyed city, a single voice called out in the night.

"Get this asshole off me!" yelled Richard. Spider tugged his blade free from the fleshless creature's eye socket and while glancing back to observe his comrade, let its body fall to the ground with the others. Richard had been forced on to his back by one of the remaining 'Skulls' and was fighting desperately to keep it from ripping him apart. Taking a moment to watch the scorched being's furious assault upon the individual, he found a small measure of enjoyment in witnessing the torment within the struggling man's eyes. On this occasion the sadistic thought proved to be only fleeting and his pragmatic side soon took hold. Without a travelling companion his journey would likely prove to be more hazardous. Upon this consideration, Spider marched up behind the disfigured creature and it let out a loud gurgle as he deftly plunged Vanja's sharp point through the back of its head.

"Thanks, dude, but what took you so long?" mumbled Richard grumpily, as he fought to push away the Skull's weighty corpse from atop him. The pair had been walking since sunrise and had barely stopped all day. To make matters worse they had now run out of food. Ignoring the man's comment, Spider continued to scour the smog-filled street and the encompassing ruins for any signs of danger. When he was satisfied they were relatively safe, he silently beckoned to Richard and wandered away down the road, with his long black coat blowing in the breeze behind him. Although curious, Richard knew better than to ask questions and dashed after his stoic companion.

After kicking a few loose planks free from a boarded up shop window, Spider slipped inside the store. Not wanting to be left alone on the dark street, Richard didn't hesitate to follow after him. Although poorly lit, they could see the interior of the store was filled with the shadows of several shelving displays and as they made their way across the creaking floor, they could hear discarded food cartons crunching underfoot. While Spider began a thorough search of the shelves, Richard decided to investigate the stock room situated at the building's rear. A rasping cough sounded from within and as he entered, two dishevelled looking men emerged from the gloom to confront him.

Remembering the harmless old man they had encountered the night before, Richard held up his hands. "Hey there, I don't want no trouble. I'm just looking for somewhere to rest up for the night." The two unkempt men looked at each other and dashed forward to strike at him with lengths of wood. When he heard Richard's pained cries, Spider vaulted over the counter to stand calmly before the attackers.

The abrupt arrival of the baleful figure gave the survivors cause to reconsider their assault upon his unconscious companion, and as Spider nonchalantly lit a cigarette they both took a step backwards. The two men looked increasingly anxious as the menacing figure smoked and studied them with quiet contemplation.

As he exhaled a cloud of smoke, he whispered, "One of you may de-part this place a-live."

"W-Which one of us?" responded one of the men fearfully, while glancing to his comrade, who was also clearly quite unnerved by the situation.

Spider's mouth revealed a wicked grin. "You de-cide."

The men looked at their intimidator blocking the only exit and then to the light glinting from the knife held ready at his side. With their confidence utterly shaken, the men immediately turned on each other. While they strangled one another on the dirty floor, Spider just stood by and finished his cigarette. After a few minutes, one of the men finally staggered to his feet, leaving his friend lying dead.

"Can-can I go?" asked the survivor, gasping for breath.

Spider dropped the cigarette butt to the floor and leaned forward to look the shorter man directly in the eye. "If I e-ver see you a-gain, you will die." The wheezing man took one glimpse at Spider's cold blue eyes and fled the room.

When Richard awoke he was lying on a pile of cardboard and found the wound to his head had been neatly bandaged. There was a small fire burning beside him and suspended over the flames was an iron pan, filled with small pieces of sizzling meat.

He looked to Spider, who was sat in the shadows beside him. "Where are those guys?"

Spider leant forward in to the flickering orange light and turned over some of the meat with his knife, before looking up at him with a slightly amused expression. "A-round."

Richard groaned as he sat up and held his head. "Thanks for the first-aid. Hey, where did you get the meat? I'm pretty damn hungry."

The man shook his head. "This is not for you."

"What the fuck, man? You're a real jerk sometimes, you know that? I mean, I know we aint exactly friends, but I thought you had my back." Spider sighed and tossed him a dented tin of food he had found on the largely empty shelves.

"What's this?" asked Richard as he picked up the can and read the tattered label. "Woofo chunks? You are seriously feeding me dog food, when you're eating steak?"

"So it would seem," replied Spider cryptically.

"Huh, guess I know where I stand then. So, is the 'black man' allowed any water?"

"This is the last of the wa-ter," explained Spider as he passed him a nearly empty plastic bottle. "I have al-ready ta-ken my share and for the re-cord the co-lour of your skin does not con-cern me."

"Fine. If that's true, what's the deal with giving me damn dog food?" asked Richard before taking a few sips of water from the bottle.

Spider gestured to the door of the small bathroom behind him. "I will do what-ever is nec-essary to sur-vive."

Richard pushed the closet door open wide and winced at the sight of a corpse lying on the tiled floor, which had been partially stripped of flesh. He recognised the body as one of the men who had attacked him only hours earlier.

"Shit, what have you done?" muttered Richard in disbelief, while looking to the pan of cooking meat. "I thought we agreed to leave the past in the past. Guess you really are just a monster like the media said."

Spider glared at him. "I would su-ggest you eat your food and get some rest. We may reach the rail tu-nnels we re-quire to-morrow."

"Sure," responded Richard brusquely. "Just so you know, I think you and I should part ways when we reach Red-Hill."

Spider stared into the dancing flames of the fire and coldly replied, "A-greed."

Richard had just finished consuming his unappetising meal and had now settled down to sleep, leaving Spider alone by the fireside.

"Just a monster," whispered Spider to himself, as he thought back to that fateful day. Once more he heard the men's laughter and his children's cries, desperately calling out for him to save them.

That was the day his family had died. That was the day he had become Spider.

Vîggo and Louisa had a beautiful wedding, but due to his ailing health, Marcus Johansson had been unable to attend the ceremony. The newlyweds had decided to take their honeymoon in a secluded lodge in Sweden and had spent the last few days of their break with Marcus at his home.

Later that year, Marcus was admitted in to hospital and given only days to live. Upon receiving this tragic news, both Vîggo and the heavily pregnant Louisa returned to Sweden to be by his bedside for his final hours. After his passing, they remained in in the country to attend the funeral and the day they had intended to return home to America, Louisa had gone in to labour. Due to a severe snowstorm, the ambulances couldn't reach them and Vîggo was forced to deliver his own children. The twins, a boy and a girl, were thankfully born without any complications. They named the girl Anya and the boy, Karl.

Due to Vîggo's well-paid medical career, he had managed to purchase one of the newly built mansion-like houses overlooking the Los Demones river, just as his beloved wife had wanted. For the next five years the four of them lived happily together in their family home without incident.

It was late October when the Mosely construction corporation first called at their doorstep. The family were offered a large amount of money to sell their property and were informed their neighbours had already been persuaded to sell. The company intended to build a billion dollar building project, to create a new mega-mall. After some thought on the matter, Vîggo and Louisa declined their offer. During the next month they were harassed daily by intimidating thugs, hired by the Mosely Corporation. The couple's attempts to get the law enforcement involved were thwarted by the newly elected state senator, Robert Mosely, who owned the construction company.

It was Christmas Eve and Vîggo was driving home late after finishing some last minute gift shopping. He parked the car on the driveway and collected the box of gifts from the trunk. As he wandered up the path to the front porch, a sense of dread ran through him. The front door was wide open and there were no lights on inside the house.

Upon stepping through the doorway he called out to his wife, "Louisa!" When he heard her scream from upstairs he dropped the gifts at his feet and sprinted to the stairwell. As he reached the steps, he received a sharp blow to the back of his head, sending him crashing to the wood floor. When he tried to rise, a second man brought a heavy boot stamping down on his head. He awoke dazed and confused to find himself tied to a lawn chair in his backyard. His face was so badly bruised, he could barely see out of his swollen eyes. As he struggled to break free, two burly men walked into view.

"Hey, don't go! You don't wanna miss the show!" laughed one of the men while pointing a baseball bat to the upstairs window. He looked to the upper floor of the house, where he was horrified to see his two children sitting on the window ledge, in their night clothes. Upon seeing their little bodies were wrapped in reels of barbed wire, Vîggo screamed, "Why are you do-ing this!"

A pallid looking man with grey hair leaned out of an upstairs window, while holding the badly beaten and naked Louisa in front of him. "Nice bitch you got here! You should have all moved out when you were told. Yer time's up, asshole!"

"Vîggo!" shrieked the woman as she was dragged over to her children.

"Let her go!" yelled Vîggo, while pulling with all his might to free his arms. An overweight dark skinned man punched him several times to the face, leaving him in a bloody mess. He could barely breathe now, yet he still couldn't stop screaming. The grey-haired man laughed as he wrapped more lengths of wire about Louisa's unclothed body. "You love yer kids don't you, missy?"

Louisa nodded whilst crying inconsolably and as the man finished tying the last of the jagged bonds about her slender frame, he gave her a grin. "You see those wires about yer body and arms? Well, they are tied to the little ones. In a moment or two, you are gonna be their gallows and the sooner you die, the better yer kids chances of living." The man proceeded to hammer nails through her feet, fixing her to the floor and both parents cried out as the two infants were pushed from the window ledge. Vîggo's screams turned to agonised sobs as the two young children thrashed about suspended at the end of the barbed wire. He watched helplessly as his family's flesh was ripped apart by the confining snares. Cascades of blood flowed from the shrieking Louisa and the infants, who continually cried out for their daddy to help them. With the weight of her two children pulling on the sharp wire, Louisa's bonds had cut deep and with one final scream her quivering body was ripped apart. Karl and Anya also now lay still, their tiny blood drenched bodies swung gently in the wind. Vîggo was choking on his own blood and tears; he was too traumatised to even speak.

When the older man walked out into the backyard, one of the men pointed at Vîggo. "What do we do with him?"

The grey-haired individual smiled as he looked down at the transfixed Vîggo, who was staring up at the dead faces of his family. "Put him in the house, he can burn with it." While one of the large thugs dragged him and the chair indoors, the other two were laughing about what they had just done. The burly man threw Vîggo down in the middle of the living room and walked across the floor to collect a large fuel can. Unknown to the thug, the rough fall had broken the lawn chair and Vîggo was now slowly clambering to his feet. On the mantel piece, barely a few feet away from him was his grandmother's knife. As the heavily built man turned around he tried to call out, but his words were silenced by Vanja's cold steel puncturing his flabby neck. The dying man gurgled and futilely clutched at his neck, before slumping to the carpeted floor.

"What the fuck?" mumbled a voice from behind and Vîggo turned about to find the grey-haired man aiming a pistol at his head. The first gunshot grazed his head, but the next two hit him hard in the chest. Vîggo's body dropped like a stone and he quickly began to lose consciousness. The pistol wielding individual looked down at Vîggo and grinned. "You know, I'd like to say this is just business, but I do enjoy my work." The laughing man departed the house, leaving the large dark skinned man drenching the room in gasoline. While lying in a pool of his own blood, only one thing drove him to keep breathing, his pure instinct to survive. With sheer force of will he slowed his breathing, to slow his blood loss and as the huge thug went to drop a struck match, he stabbed his knife into the back of his leg, piercing an artery. The inflicted wound caused the man to fall down and as he dropped, Vîggo struck again, this time to the man's groin. Causing this man excruciating pain felt good and he hardly noticed the gasoline fuelled blaze which had ensued all about him. Despite his severe wounds, two things drove him to crawl from the burning building, his grandmother's survival teachings and a new found deep-rooted desire to inflict pain unto others. By the time he reached the front porch, his clothes and hair were aflame. The willowy man fell down the front steps, rolled on to the cool wet grass and lay there gasping for breath. In the distance he could hear the sirens of approaching emergency vehicles. They were too late, his family were already dead and Vîggo Hellstrom had died with them.

Chapter Thirteen

"City Of Graves"

Her hands were covered with stinging cuts and grazes, but she continued to dig, while trying her best to not consider the hole's grim purpose. The thick toxic smog had once more darkened the sky above and as she rolled her brother's bloody remains into the shallow grave, inhuman shrieks echoed from within the mist. Quickly covering Claude's body as best she could, the woman turned to run, but found herself being approached by several revolting skeletal beings. While hissing and grasping at the air before them with their bony hands, the milky-eyed mutants dashed forward to devour their prey. In desperation, Angeline pried a long rusty pole out from the rubble at her feet and using both hands, proceeded to wildly swing the improvised weapon in an effort to keep the disgusting monsters at bay. Her attempt to dissuade the hungry Skulls initially worked, but much to her dismay her wretched attackers soon spread out to advance on her from all sides. The heavy metal bar resonated with a dull clang as it connected with the nearest mutant's head, but the others were undeterred and rushed eagerly forward to feast on her flesh. Faced with the inevitability of death, Angeline fell to her knees, threw back her head and screamed to the heavens. The very instant the loathsome creatures reached the forlorn woman a deafening growl sounded from the ridge above. A huge mass of white fur and pointed fangs fell upon the pack of Skulls, scattering them across the hilltop. Before Angeline even knew what she was doing, she had grabbed hold of the thick ruff at the Howler's neck and climbed on to its back. The beast let out a howl as if in approval and proceeded to effortlessly bound down the steep concrete slopes to the valley below. She was once more at the Howler's den, but a vast quantity of the wreckage above had recently subsided, leaving the creature's habitat lost within the tons of debris. Whilst still astride the beast, Angeline patted the giant wolf on the head, making the animal let out a little whine.

"Perhaps you should come with me after all," whispered the woman softly. Angeline wondered if she could perhaps direct the creature's movements whilst sat upon its back and lightly kicked her left heel twice into the Howler's flank, much as she had done when riding horses as a child. The wolf turned left in apparent confusion and she ruffled the fur between its ears to commend its action. Over the next few hours, she repeated the process whilst the creature walked about the valley floor. Although the beast let out a few irritated growls from time to time, the huge animal had soon determined when she wished to turn, or move forward. Getting the massive white-furred beast to stop however, had so far proved quite problematic. After dismounting, she gulped down some water from one of the large plastic bottles and poured the remaining liquid into an

old upturned hubcap for the Howler. The animal immediately began to fervently lap up the water and whilst it was drinking, Angeline sat down to gather her thoughts.

Her simple minded brother, who she had looked after for so many years, was gone. Was she to blame? Could she have done something to stop all this? No, the blame fell solely upon those bastards Drake and Carter, but with Claude gone, Angeline found her life now held little purpose. As she thought back to happier times she had spent with her brother, the familiar thought of suicide loomed in her mind. One single desire pushed those thoughts aside, a need for revenge. The Howler, who had now finished drinking, turned and gently nudged her face, as if concerned.

Although the huge wolf's affections nearly knocked her over, they caused the sombre woman to break into a smile. *"I guess we should give you a name, non?"* Seemingly answering her, the beast suddenly grizzled, stretched and lay down flat beside her. While blinking occasionally, the Howler's blue eyes stared at her with bewilderment as she pondered a suitable name for her new companion. Angeline had always wanted a house pet, such as a cat or dog, but she couldn't because of her special brother. When they were both quite young, their father had presented Claude with a pet rabbit, but Benji bunny had been smothered to death by Claude's 'affections' within a day. She recalled having spent hours that day trying to convince her oblivious brother to release the crushed animal's body from his loving embrace. That had been one of the few days she had lost her temper with him, she had called him names like 'freak' and 'imbécile'. Claude had not understood why his big sister was so angry and it quickly resulted in him having one of his lengthy tantrums. She found herself absent-mindedly running a hand through the Howler's thick fur and turned her head to admire the animal's beautiful bright white coat.

"How about Lily?" remarked the woman as she stood up. During the next few minutes Angeline repeatedly called out the name, in the hope her companion would begin to understand her new given name. The large beast just yawned at first, but eventually responded to the woman's voice and pawed at her face, as if asking, 'Are you in pain?'

Angeline giggled. *"Ah, Lily, perhaps we can try this again later, d'accord?"* She gave Lily a brief hug and proceeded to carefully climb on to her back. As before the creature didn't seem to mind and once she felt the rider's heels gently nudging at her flanks, Lily broke in to a sprint, westwards through the desolate canyon. Angeline had now tied a length of torn cloth about her lower face in a bid to keep out the choking smog and as she rode the charging beast further into the city ruins, the fog grew dense. She was concerned for Lily, but if the Howler was even remotely suffering, she showed no sign of it. Curiously enough, Lily appeared to be enjoying herself and as they reached the end of the valley, Angeline glanced back to the distant mound where her brother was buried.

"Au revoir, Claude, I shall miss you," she whispered.

Quickly wiping the tears from her eyes, she clung on tightly to the hulking animal as it dashed up the steep embankment of twisted wreckage. As they sped through the mist-filled ruins at the heart of the city, the woman observed a vast amount of decaying corpses. A great number of the bodies were lifeless scorched carcasses, victims of the solar flare and the ensuing chaos. However, Angeline could also perceive an alarming amount of dishevelled figures, staggering within the toxic shroud, all seeking their next meal of living flesh. The horrific sight of so many men, women and children irrevocably changed by the virus made her feel violently sick. Wanting to be far from this nightmarish place, she spurred Lily to race onwards and having sensed the hordes of hungry Infected, the beast seemed happy to oblige. They continued their journey until the sun had set, by now the Howler's pace had greatly slowed and she was panting heavily.

Angeline felt guilty for having pushed the poor creature so hard and gently stroked the fur between her ears. *"I am sure we will find somewhere to rest soon, Lily."* What they desperately needed now was a shelter, but all she could see in the surrounding gloom was endless piles of debris that had once been towering office buildings and people's homes. She had no doubt that if they stopped to rest out here in the open air, they wouldn't survive the night. Lily pushed onwards, but her weary run soon dwindled to a slow walk and Angeline began to become frantic with worry. The Howler suddenly growled and unexpectedly bounded forward with such break-neck speed the woman slipped from the wolf's back. Although she had sustained a few nasty bruises from the fall, she wasn't badly hurt and swiftly picked herself up from the rocky ground to give chase after

Lily. Night had fallen over the city and she could barely see more than a few feet ahead. Despite wanting to call out for the Howler, she remained quiet. Even a single cry could bring an Infected horde rushing to feed upon her and here in the darkness she would have little chance to defend herself. Feeling utterly helpless, she jogged blindly onwards into the blackness. Each step she took into the unknown caused her to become increasingly afraid. Venturing through the tall maze-like piles of jagged rocks, she swore she could hear unseen beings stirring all about her. Focusing all her thoughts upon finding Lily, the distraught woman pressed on. When she heard a familiar growl murmuring from somewhere above, Angeline couldn't resist calling out for the beast. Feeling the embankment of dirt before her, she scrambled up the slippery mud slope, while constantly praying she would be reunited with Lily at the summit. Halfway up the slope she felt a heavy tug on her leg. Glancing down she was terrified to see a ghoulish one-armed figure gripping hold of her ankle with its bony hand, while its jaw snapped at the heel of her boot. Recoiling in disgust, Angeline dug her fingers deep in to the dirt and using her free leg, kicked down to strike the Infected in the head. The sickening result was much like that of a rotten egg being smashed.

The creature's skull cracked apart in to a dozen fragments, while the remnants of its brain burst like a pus-filled abscess over her boot.

"Gross!" exclaimed the woman grimacing with absolute revulsion and began once more to scale the embankment

before her. At the crest of the slope she was met by the gruesome sound of tearing flesh. Drawing the stiletto dagger from the sheath on her inner thigh, she stayed in a crouched position and silently advanced towards the origin of the noise. In the clearing before her she was relieved to see Lily, who was happily dining on a fresh kill. While the beast was occupied with ripping off parts of the giant Vermin to eat, Angeline stealthily moved up beside her. The woman's stomach rumbled just at the thought of food and couldn't resist cutting out a sizeable chunk of meat from the animal's flank. The huge wolf didn't seem to mind sharing its kill with her and just continued to bolt down its bloody meal.

"At least it's not human," whispered Angeline, trying to console herself about eating meat from a giant rodent. She decided to wait to find a place to cook the meat, as she couldn't bear the thought of eating it raw. At that moment the clouds overhead briefly parted and the moonlight revealed a partially standing apartment block, merely a minutes' walk from them.

"Come on, Lily, this way," said Angeline, urging her companion to follow. The beast ignored her at first and just continued to gnaw on the rapidly diminishing carcass. After a few more calls, the Howler decided to drag it's kill over to the woman now waiting at the building's entrance. Only the ground floor appeared to be intact and upon forcing the door open, she was surprised to find a skinny old man sound asleep on the grimy floor. Lily seemed reluctant to come inside at first, but with Angeline's encouragement the large animal soon squeezed itself through the doorway, while

dragging its food along with it. While the Howler sat down in a corner and continued to strip the last of the meat from the Vermin's bones, Angeline bent down to wake the scruffy old man.

He coughed and spluttered as he rose from the floor, then stared up at her with an odd calm. "You're a lot better lookin' than the last four."

"The last four?" enquired Angeline mystified.

"The last two men were mean. I hid when I saw 'em. One of 'em only had one eye. The grey-haired one killed a boy and cut him up for food," grumbled the man while flinching at the horrid memory. "The man actually seemed to enjoy hurting the poor kid."

"Drake and Carter," muttered Angeline, while shaking her head in disgust. *"Who were the other two you met before them?"*

The old man gave her a toothless grin as he paused to think. "One was a black feller, seemed quite nice too. The tall pale one had cold eyes and wore a long black coat. Can't say I liked the look of him." At that point the frail man spotted the large shape of the Howler curled up in the corner next to the Vermin's skeletal remains and began to panic.

"Monsters in the pantry!" squealed the man whilst pointing at the sleeping beast.

"It is all right, she won't hurt you," explained Angeline trying to calm the manic individual. After making humming noises and rolling his eyes, he suddenly broke in to a song, causing Lily to awaken. Fortunately the tired wolf just

dismissed the raving madman and settled back down to sleep.

"Are you quite all right, monsieur?"

"If we are all friends…" – the man went silent and danced on the spot for a moment, before whispering to her in a conspiratorial manner – "you should have a present!" The man babbled to himself excitedly as he hobbled over to a shopping cart over-laden with random junk. While the crazy man rummaged through the numerous oddities in his cart, Angeline noticed the dwindling flames of a small campfire where the man had been sleeping. After rekindling the fire, she grabbed the iron pan from her rucksack and began to cook the large slab of sinewy vermin meat. The old man was now having an animated discussion with himself and had placed a tinfoil hat on his balding head.

Eventually he pulled an object from his collection and placed it proudly at her feet, while mumbling, "Search and rescue." Angeline looked down at the sackcloth bag with suspicion while she ate some of the chewy steak. When she had eaten her fill, she wrapped up the remaining food in a piece of cloth and placed it in her bag. The old man looked on eagerly as she picked up his gift and opened the sack. She half expected to find something disgusting inside, but instead found herself holding a flare-gun. The pistol was in good working order and amazingly there was also a small plastic box containing a number of phosphorous flares.

She turned to the man and nodded in appreciation. *"Merci, monsieur, this will be very helpful."*

The man held up a hand to his straggly beard and chuckled to himself, "Search and rescue." When he saw his fire was burning brightly again, he joyfully tapped the tinfoil hat on his head in triumph, laughed and once more lay down by his makeshift hearth.

After taking several sips of water from the bottle, she poured the rest in to the iron pan for Lily. As she sat back down beside her furry companion on the hardwood floor, she thought back to the traumatic events of the last few days.

Perhaps tomorrow she would confront her brother's killers, but what of the men they had been hunting? They had apparently murdered a priest back in the town of Chastity, but if that was true, why had they not harmed this old man? She decided to put the matter out of her mind and get some rest. Maybe tomorrow she would get some answers; maybe tomorrow she would avenge her brother's death.

Chapter Fourteen

"Mines & Tunnels"

After donning their gas-masks, the two men exited the convenience store and stepped out into the cool morning air. Once back on the street, they became quickly aware of the change in the weather. Although the encompassing mists were lighter today, it was now pouring down with rain and they were soon splashing their way through the rivers of dirty puddles forming on the damaged roadway. Spider had noted that his travelling companion had been oddly quiet since their discussion the previous night and judging by the fearful looks he had been giving him, he decided it may soon be necessary to terminate their relationship.

"When we get to the town, we part ways, no hard feelings, okay?" said Richard, who was trying to ease the obvious tension between them.

Spider glanced back at the man and gestured to their bleak surroundings. "You may leave when-ever you wish."

After considering the miles of sprawling ruins all around them, Richard sheepishly replied, "Well man, let's just keep moving, yeah?"

"Of course," answered Spider in a hushed tone of voice. They journeyed onwards for the next few hours in silence. On several occasions they found groups of rotting Infected wandering in their path, but each time Spider managed to discern an alternate route, bypassing the hostile beings. As they progressed westwards, they noticed there were a great deal fewer Infected in this region and as they traversed the curiously open stretch of road, Richard suddenly froze. He had just heard a faint beep from beneath his right foot and with trepidation called out, "Oh sh-shit, man, I think I'm standing on a mine!"

Spider stopped in his tracks and looked back to the motionless man, who was visibly sweating with fear. "That is most re-grett-able."

"Please do something!" implored Richard shaking with fright. He watched as Spider sat down cross-legged on the concrete, pulled off his gas-mask and placed a cigarette between his lips.

"What the hell are you doing? We are in a fucking mine field!" screamed the distressed man. "For God's sake help me!" Spider smiled at him and lit the cigarette with the lighter he had just collected from his pocket. While smoking, he remained quiet and surveyed the scene before him with an eerie calm.

"What the hell are you waiting for, man?" yelled Richard, becoming increasingly agitated.

Spider was considering his options. He had spotted a handful of mines dotted along this stretch of road and was fairly certain he could avoid them. However, dealing with his comrade's predicament could cost him dearly and in truth he wasn't even sure what he could do to aid him. With his decision now made, he stood up, replaced the mask to his face and walked away into the mist.

"You can't just leave me here!" cried Richard. "Pl-please for pity's sake, help me!" A few minutes passed and the traumatised man had spent that time staring at the dull red glow emanating from beneath his shoe.

"Maybe it won't go off? Maybe it's actually a dud?" mumbled Richard and shifted his free leg, in preparation to lift his foot from the explosive.

"Not a good i-dea," said Spider, who was now standing beside him.

"You-you came back?" stammered the man. "I thought you'd left me for dead." Spider showed him a bemused smile and held up the sheet of metal he had found.

"What you doing with that?" asked Richard, as his companion squatted down by his feet. He didn't answer and rather confusingly he appeared to be inspecting his shoe.

"Do not move," instructed Spider, as he retrieved Vanja from his coat pocket.

Richard's eyes stared at the sharp knife with uneasiness, "Oh God, you're not going to cut my foot off are you?"

"Your foot would pro-vide in-su-fficient weight to pre-vent the detona-tion," replied Spider, slightly amused by the man's remark. Using Vanja's tip, he pierced the man's leather shoe just above the sole and slowly cut around the circumference of the footwear. A small amount of blood seeped from the tear, but thankfully Richard managed to not flinch, or move his foot. Cutting away the upper covering, he exposed the man's foot on the detached rubber sole.

"This is the diff-icult part," commented Spider dourly, as he began to ease the thin metal panel between the foot and the remainder of the shoe. After several excruciating minutes, he had forced the metal directly under the foot and swiftly set about piling bricks on either side of the exposed metal. Upon completing this task, he immediately retreated to a safe distance and called out, "Lift your foot from the de-vice slow-ly and run to me."

The trembling Richard hesitated for a few seconds and screwed up his eyes as he dared to raise his bare foot from the metal. Spider looked on with intrigue as the man sprinted towards him with all the speed he could humanly muster.

He had made it about half the distance, when there was a deafening explosion and the force of the blast sent Richard barrelling forward into Spider. The two men lay sprawled on the concrete, as a heavy shower of dirt and stones rained down all around them. Climbing back to his feet, Richard turned to thank the man, but found Spider scowling and holding his hands up in visible surrender.

"We have com-pany," remarked Spider, sounding annoyed.

Once Richard saw the six armed men advancing on them from within the ruins, he sighed and raised his hands. "Hey, on the bright side I guess this day can only get better, right?"

Spider took one glimpse at the snarling gunmen bearing down on them and shook his head. "Doubt-ful."

Angeline was awoken at daybreak by the patter of water against glass and got up to take a look. Peering out of the entrance's water-streaked window at the rain, she was pleased to see the dense fog had mostly lifted; it would make traversing the city a great deal easier. Looking around the lobby she could see no sign of the old man. At first she thought the crazy guy must have departed during the night, but upon hearing a faint snoring from a cupboard under the stairs, she knew that wasn't the case. Angeline wandered over to the closet, opened the door and was taken aback by what she found. The old man had turned the surprisingly spacious cupboard in to a rather cosy little bedroom. He was sound asleep on a tattered bedroll, with his precious trolley of junk beside him. It looked like the poor soul had been staying here for some time. Had he been living here before the event? One other thing caught her attention, there was a dripping pipe running up the back wall and beneath it was a bucket containing a large quantity of clean looking water. The woman had been considering leaving the dotty man some water, but now knew it would not be necessary.

"Au revoir, monsieur," murmured Angeline, and gently shut the door. Lily was now awake and had begun pacing about the lobby. The woman sat on the dusty floor and ate some of the large Vermin steak she had cooked the night before. As she washed it down with a few mouthfuls of water, she noticed Lily had been watching her eat. The huge

wolf was holding its head on one side as if to say, 'So where's my food?'

"Ah, je suis dèsolé, Lily," said Angeline apologising and tossed her the sizeable chunk of remaining meat. Lily caught it in her jaws, chewed it up and in an instant it was gone. The placid beast seemed content with her offering and returned to pacing about the floor.

A few minutes later, Angeline was holding on tightly to the Howler's back as it charged effortlessly between the mounds of rocks and numerous car wrecks. Riding through the ruins at such velocity on the massive animal felt truly exhilarating and despite the grim surroundings, the woman couldn't help but smile. She had always enjoyed riding horses as a child, but this was something else entirely. After an hour of frantic travel, Lily stopped for a much needed rest and Angeline offered her panting companion a pan of water. While the Howler gulped down the refreshing liquid, the woman climbed to the peak of a nearby hill to scout ahead and what she saw caused her heart to sink. The edge of the city was in sight, but the toxic or perhaps even radioactive cloud banks were even heavier beyond the city's boundaries. How could she and Lily hope to survive passing through that horrendous smog? The sound of an explosion abruptly echoed on the wind and scouring the horizon she could make out wisps of black smoke rising in the distance. On impulse she ran back down to Lily, collected her belongings and vaulted on to the beast's back. She soon found the cause of the explosion, judging by the smoking crater, someone or something had set off a mine. Wanting to avoid detonating any more of the lethal devices, she steered Lily to scale a nearby slope and had her run along the high ground overlooking the street. They followed the ridge for about a mile and when Angeline heard gunshots, she brought Lily to a hasty halt. Down in the valley below she spied a large cluster of tents and dozens of rowdy well-armed men. Some of their group were just returning to the camp and appeared to have two others held hostage at gunpoint. The woman strained her eyes in the half-light to get a better look at the captives. One of the men was dark skinned and the other man was wearing a long black coat. These were the individuals the old man at the apartment building had spoken of. Knowing Carter and Drake's exceptional tracking skills, they would likely not be far behind her. Carter in particular had an insatiable appetite for cruelty and he'd undoubtedly make some sort of horrid deal to purchase those two hostages. Taking a minute to look around the surroundings hills, she noticed a large rail tunnel situated at the end of the valley, not far from the encampment. Why would these people risk camping so closely to a place which was a potential haven for all sorts of dangerous creatures? She wondered. Then it dawned upon her, the mists were virtually non-existent here. Clean air must be blowing from the tunnel and that meant there must be a way out of the city. She watched the two captives disappear from view, as they were forcibly pushed inside one of the larger tents. Her desire for revenge suddenly seemed quite unattainable, it was obvious that she would have no chance of killing Carter and Drake here. For the first time since her brother's death, Angeline wasn't sure what to do. Should she try to rescue those men and spare them a painful death at the hands of Carter? Or should she just take the opportunity to escape the city and attempt to flee through the tunnel with Lily?

As she deliberated, there was a commotion in the camp below, it seemed her 'old friends' from the farm had just arrived at the camp. Unlike the other two men, they were clearly known to them and accepted with open arms. Angeline scowled as she observed the two hated men laughing and drinking with all their apparent friends. She had made her decision; tonight she would have her revenge.

Chapter Fifteen

"Rose Amongst Thorns"

Night had fallen over the camp and within a canvas tent, two captives lay on the dirt floor with their arms bound tightly behind their backs. A small log fire was crackling between them, bathing the pair in a dull orange light. Spider had been observing his fraught companion, who continued to fidget about in the vague hope of loosening his bonds. The possibility of escape appeared to be remote, there were dozens of men waiting outside and to make matters worse, they had seized most of their belongings. However, their captors had neglected to remove his leather coat and had failed to notice the throwing dagger he had concealed in his boot prior to their capture. Having already severed his bindings with the small blade, he had now angled his body to face the tent's entrance. The next person to enter through that doorway would feel his dagger's point piercing their heart.

The darkness cloaked her appearance well, but regardless she took great care to keep her distance from the multiple large bonfires burning about the camp. As she navigated a path through the groups of men situated amidst the various tents, the scent of alcohol and stale sweat hung heavy in the air. A majority of the men here were quite obviously drunk, high or both and upon seeing the plethora of used hypodermic needles littering the area, she relaxed a little. It was now clear that most of these men would be barely able to stand, so the chances of them recognising her as an intruder were slim. Angeline was thankful she had chosen to leave Lily at the entrance to the rail tunnel; even these heavily inebriated individuals wouldn't fail to spot a huge white wolf traipsing about their camp. In truth, Lily had seemed happy to keep away from this place; perhaps she had been wary of their numbers. On the other hand, maybe it had something to do with the numerous severed heads that adorned the tips of the tent poles. A few of them had belonged to Howler's, while others looked to be from giant insects, or other unknown grotesque creatures, which so far she had been fortunate enough not to encounter. Now nearing the heart of the encampment, she grimaced at the sight of several naked and badly beaten women, who were lying sprawled in some of the smaller tents. The women varied greatly in age, but all shared one thing in common, they were all strung out on drugs. Masses of septic needle marks covered their bare bodies and most of them were calling out, begging for their next fix. Feeling utterly sickened, Angeline was tempted to put some of these poor girls out of their misery, but she had a more pressing task to achieve. Upon reaching the tent she had been seeking, she took a deep breath and stepped inside.

The entrance flaps parted and as the slender figure bent down to enter, a brief whistling sounded as a projectile was thrown through the air.

There was a dull thud as the dagger found its mark and the victim clutched at the painful injury to their chest, before falling to the dirt. Seeing the body was only halfway inside the tent, Spider grabbed hold of the body's long hair and proceeded to drag the corpse in to the interior. Rolling the corpse on to its back, he briefly paused to look at the cadaver, before searching through their possessions. Sadly the old man had held nothing of value and he turned his attention to his bound comrade. He knelt down beside Richard and cut his bindings. "You are wel-come to de-part if you wish."

"Thanks," responded the man, still quite confused by what had just happened. "Wait a minute, you mean you're not leaving?"

"I re-quire my po-ssessions," whispered Spider.

"Forget that stuff, man, let's just get out of here", said Richard rubbing his sore wrists. "Anyway, there must be dozens of tents out there, how you gonna find the right one?"

Spider's mouth now wore a familiar sinister grin. "Per-haps I should dis-cuss it with one of our hosts."

Richard tiptoed over to the exit to leave, but when he saw the crowds of rowdy men lurking all about him, he immediately reconsidered, "Fine, I'll just wait here. Just don't be too long, okay?"

Spider peered cautiously out from the doorway to survey the surroundings and glanced back to his nervous companion. "I doubt you will re-ceive any-more visi-tors while I am gone. The men seem su-fficient-ly dis-tracted."

"Let's hope so. Good luck." Spider gave him a nod and disappeared into the night.

Angeline was certain she had seen one of the two men she had been seeking enter this abode, yet oddly there was no-one here. Judging by the copious heaps of items lying about the place she determined this was likely the leader's dwelling. There were huge wads of dollars piled high on a nearby desk and beneath it she could see a rusty metal safe. As Angeline squatted down to inspect it, she heard brisk footsteps approaching from behind and before she could move, she had been pulled backwards to the floor. While on her back, she received a flurry of weighty punches to the face.

Drake's smirking face bore down on her and laughed as the concussed woman feebly struggled to free herself. "Hola, bitch, I is gonna fuck you bad and when I am done with you, I will cut out those pretty green eyes with your own blade. Just think, the last thing you will get to see is me using you!"

The disorientated Angeline felt the dagger being drawn from her inner thigh and winced in pain as it was used to rip open her clothes from chest to groin. She managed to summon the strength to push him away, but this just spurred Drake to strike her once more in the face. As she faded in and out of consciousness, she felt her legs being forced apart. Drake's calloused hands grabbed hold of her exposed breasts and as he manoeuvred himself on top of her, drool from his protruding tongue dripped on to her bare body. The man's stinking breath was inexplicably replaced by a shower of blood and Angeline thought it must somehow be her own. The copious flow of crimson liquid splattered on to her face, leaving her virtually blind, but the weight of Drake's body was suddenly no longer bearing down on her. A constant agonised gurgling sounded from beside her and with an effort she wiped the grime from her eyes to take a look. Rolling on the floor next to her in excruciating pain was Drake, blood was streaming from his open mouth, but oddly he wasn't screaming. A tall figure in a long black coat stood silhouetted against the flames of the camp fire burning at the centre of the tent. Angeline watched as the pale-skinned man forced Drake's arms behind his back and tied them with a length of thick rope. The stranger's gaunt face and chiselled jaw made him a little ghoulish in appearance, but Angeline found him strangely handsome. The man turned his cold blue eyes from his blood vomiting victim, to look at her and gave her a small smile.

For a moment Spider thought he had once more laid eyes upon his beloved Louisa. With her long golden hair and sparkling green eyes, this woman before him was indeed much like his departed wife. He noted that despite her injuries and state of undress, she remained quite beautiful. Spider blinked in puzzlement at his own thoughts and returned his focus back to his latest prey. He had already spotted his possessions scattered amongst the piles of clutter in the corner and promptly retrieved Vanja from a basket filled with various blades.

"Pardon, monsieur, but who are you?" asked Angeline, as she staggered over to a heap of clothing, to pick out some new clothes. The man remained silent as he lit a cigarette and continued to quietly observe the panicking Drake, choking on his own blood.

"My name is Angeline. May I ask, what did you do to him?" enquired the woman, as she finished getting dressed.

"I re-moved his tongue," answered the man tersely. "You may call me Spi-der."

"D'accord, I cannot place your accent, where are you from?" she asked trying to strike up conversation, in an attempt to ascertain if this man could be trusted.

"Swe-den. I would suggest you leave," replied Spider in a hushed tone, as he hauled the retching Drake over to the fire.

Angeline was rather confused by her rescuer's words. *"If you are intending to leave the city, may I travel with you?"* Spider didn't seem to be listening and was now busy tying the ropes hanging from the tent beams overhead, about Drake's arms. *"You intend to burn him alive?"* commented Angeline, somewhat shocked.

"Is that a prob-lem for you?" responded Spider, while concentrating on the task at hand.

The woman barely paused for thought before replying, *"Non, he is a bastard. Let him burn."*

Spider looked at her with new found intrigue. "If you wish to a-ccompa-ny me, head to the third blue tent to your right. If there is a grum-py black man wait-ing in-side, you will have found the co-rrect place."

"Handsome and funny," said the woman managing a small smile. As she departed, Angeline couldn't resist taking one last look at the struggling Drake being hoisted above the flames. She left the tent with a broad smile on her face; revenge was sweet, one down, one to go.

Spider watched the speechless man thrash about in pain as the fire's intense heat burnt away the flesh from his lower body. He had purposefully hauled him to such a height, that the individual would be unlikely to die from the ordeal, but by the time the fires had dwindled, the man would have lost his legs and whatever had been between them. Satisfied that the burning man's fate was sealed, he turned his attention to the safe beneath the desk. It was unlocked and inside he was a little taken aback to discover a multitude of eyeless doll heads. Upon spying a small metal box laid on the lower shelf, he carefully opened it and within he found a glass vial of glowing blue liquid. Printed along the length of the glass was a long series of numbers and the word 'Diamondinium'. After studying the strange substance for a few moments, he placed the vial in his holdall and with Vanja ready in hand, he crept back out into the gloom.

When he returned to his travelling companions, it appeared that Richard had thought Angeline to be one of their captors and had attempted to hit her with a log. The man was still holding his groin and wincing, but they were both clearly keen to follow him out of the encampment. Their departure proved trickier than Spider had anticipated. It seemed more men had arrived at the camp and he was forced to slit the throat of two patrolling sentries before they made their eventual escape.

As they reached the tunnel entrance, a huge white-furred Howler emerged from the darkness to block their path. Richard let out a short scream in fright and just as Spider was reaching for his sawn-off shotgun, Angeline rushed forward to greet it.

Spider watched with fascination as she gave the creature a big hug and climbed on to its back. He smiled to himself, this Angeline was truly an extraordinary woman, travelling with her and her furry friend would likely prove most interesting.

Chapter Sixteen

"Following The Tracks"

In the early hours of the morning, the two men stared up at the legless charred figure suspended above the smouldering campfire. Carter had known Drake a long time and was infuriated that such an adept ally had been taken from him. The shirtless brute of a man by his side was called 'Razor', he was the leader of this survivor group and Carter knew him well. Although the man was a fearsome fighter, his mind was ravaged by madness and that made him rather unpredictable. He had changed his appearance quite radically since they had last met, his muscular body was now covered in tribal tattoos and his head was virtually shaved, leaving only a long spiky Mohican, which he plastered upright with the blood from his victims. Drake was still alive, but barely. Most of his remaining skin resembled a gruesome collage of crimson blisters and despite the fact his tongue had been cut out, he was desperately trying to tell him something.

Carter quickly tired of the man's unintelligible pained roaring. "Shut your damn mouth, you fool! I'm sick of you spittin' yer blood and drool over me! Now I'm gonna ask you some questions and you blink that workin' eye of yours, once for yes and twice for no, got it?" Drake closed his seeing eye once to show he understood.

"Enough of this FUCKING BULLSHIT!" yelled Razor, who then stormed across the tent floor to look in the open safe, while muttering to himself. "They TOOK my prized possession, KILLED three of my guys, and super-crispy-fried this ugly fuck! What's that you say? We should hunt the assholes down? They went through the tunnels, right?" Carter looked on with concern as the psychotic man began a lengthy exchange of words with the plastic doll heads in the safe. While Razor was engrossed in conversation, Carter asked Drake a series of simple questions and when he asked if the two men they had been tracking were still alone, he was shocked by the man's response.

A stream of blood poured from Drake's mouth as he forced a single distorted word from his lips, "ANN-GE-LIIINE."

Carter's eyes narrowed. "I'll see she pays along with the others."

"KIILL MEE," rasped Drake, causing more blood to splutter from his mouth and dribble down his chin.

The old man looked down at the pistols on his belt and shook his head. "You aint worth the bullet, son. Anyhow, I reckon these guys will be carving you up for meat soon enough." He gave his distraught, wheezing ally a dismissive salute farewell and wandered over to Razor, who had begun head-butting the safe, while screaming obscenities.

"So, you got a plan in mind?" asked Carter, expecting a nonsensical reply from the deranged psycho. The manic individual tilted his bleeding head to cast him an angry sideways glance. His cold unblinking eyes stared at him with apparent malicious intent and just as Carter was contemplating reaching for his guns; Razor's hateful expression broke into an insane grin.

"Oh, WE'VE got a plan!" said Razor laughing maniacally. "You, me and a bunch of my boys are going in those tunnels to HUNT those fuckers down!"

"Strategy was never really one of your talents, was it?" replied Carter with a wry smile. "So, when do we leave?" Razor stood up to his full height and with a single flex of his corded muscles, hurled a hatchet across the room. There was a sickening crunch as the weapon's heavy blade split Drake's skull apart.

He sneered at the dangling corpse and turned to one of his men waiting at the tent's entrance. "Get that dead bitch hacked up for food and tell the others we leave within the hour. WE ARE GOIN' TO TOWN, BOYS!"

The concrete walls of the rail tunnel seemed to stretch on forever and there was no discernible way to tell just how far they had actually travelled. Knowing they couldn't risk waiting for the light of dawn, they walked blindly onwards into the pitch black, until fatigue finally took its toll. Up ahead there was a red phosphorescent sign marking an entrance to a maintenance office and Spider considered it may prove a suitable place to rest. While he and Angeline went to investigate, the anxious Richard reluctantly waited in the cold tunnels with the woman's large Howler. Spider pushed the metal door; it swung open with a discordant creak and with their blades in hand, they stepped through the doorway into the dismal chamber. The air inside was particularly foul and while Spider swiftly equipped his gas-mask, Angeline began to retch violently on the noxious odour. Richard had felt uneasy standing around with the giant wolf eyeing him and when he saw Angeline crawling from the office on all fours, he rushed over to help. As he reached the choking woman, she began to vomit and he took a few steps back.

"You all right, girl?" asked the man sounding concerned. "Where's Spider?"

Angeline coughed repeatedly and pointed behind her to the entrance, where he could see strange gaseous vapours drifting from within.

"Oh man," said Richard screwing up his face in disgust, "What's making that god-awful stink?"

Upon hearing unsteady footsteps from a nearby connecting hallway, Spider immediately backed himself into a corner.

He waited silently in the darkness, poised to strike with his knife. His eyes had begun to adjust to the constant gloom and he could now make out some of his surroundings. The small office's floor was littered with stacks of old boxes and directly opposite him there appeared to be a short corridor leading to another doorway. He quietly observed as a single figure slowly shuffled towards him from the lightless passageway. Spider had encountered several forms of the Infected since the event and was not particularly phased to see this walking corpse spewing poisonous fumes. Whilst he was wearing a gas-mask, this wretched creature likely posed no greater danger than the many others he had dealt with. When the Infected was within striking distance, he darted forward and thrust Vanja through one of its blood-weeping eyes. As he yanked the blade free from the eye socket, the fetid being gurgled and fell dead. Looking down at the creature, Spider began to wonder if the virus had affected all the population differently, or more worryingly, whether the Damocles virus was still in fact mutating. He felt a sudden painful sensation in his right arm and was aghast to see another rotting Infected had its jaws clamped around the sleeve of his leather coat. Having been lost in his thoughts, he had failed to notice the foul being stirring amidst the piles of cardboard boxes and on reaction tried to kick the creature away. As he raised his foot, the Infected lashed out at him with such force that he was sent tumbling over the containers behind him. While the man lay dazed on his back, the voracious corpse lurched forward to bite his exposed neck. When he saw the decaying creature diving towards him, he realised Vanja was no longer in his grasp and instinctively reached for the throwing knife in his pocket. As his attacker grabbed hold of him, he jammed the small blade into the side of its skull, but much to Spider's disappointment, the revolting monster continued to bear down on him. While he fought to keep it from tearing out his throat, a loud metallic chime suddenly rang out and the Infected fell into a crumpled heap beside him. Richard offered him a helping hand up from the floor and as he was pulled to his feet, Spider stared quizzically at the familiar heavy iron pan held in the man's hand.

Spider glanced at the corpse and back to Richard, quite bemused. "Apparent-ly not just for cook-ing."

Richard shrugged. "Yeah, I looked in your bag. It was either this, or the shotgun and I couldn't find any shells for the gun."

"Your in-terven-tion was most help-ful," commented Spider, as he collected Vanja and the throwing knife which was still lodged in the Infected's skull.

Richard shuffled his feet uneasily. "Look man, I don't really trust you, but that don't mean I want you dead."

"Most touch-ing," said Spider smiling. "And how is our lady friend?"

"I am okay," whispered Angeline softly from the doorway. *"If the place is now safe, perhaps we can now rest here, non?"* Spider nodded, and with Richard's assistance, they proceeded to drag the two bodies out into the rail tunnel. Not long after they had all settled down in the office to get some much needed rest. Lily was clearly unhappy being cooped up in such a small room, but Angeline knew that after a drink of water and a short sleep, the beast would likely be better tempered. Richard had already fallen asleep on a pile of boxes and was snoring loudly.

Angeline shot him a look of annoyance and turned to look at Spider, who had just lit a small fire using some of the old boxes. *"Please tell me you do not also snore."*

Spider sat down and leant against a wall. "I do not know. I rare-ly sleep any-more and I us-ually travel a-lone."

Despite their tiredness, Angeline and Spider spent the next hour in conversation. She told him about her brother, the farm where they had found shelter and her need for revenge on the man named Carter. Spider seemed undaunted by her words and confirmed he had been the one who had killed her acquaintances at the farm. Angeline was troubled to hear what had transpired with the priest at Chastity, but by Spider's account it seemed that man had actually deserved to die. When Angeline revealed she had resorted to eating human flesh to survive, Spider was oddly sympathetic. The man had calmly told her that he had done many questionable things in the pursuit of survival.

"So may I ask why you are going to Red-hill?" enquired Angeline.

Spider sighed. "My fam-ily was mur-dered sev-eral years a-go and re-cent-ly I re-ceived in-for-mation that my wife is still a-live."

"I see. Who told you this?"

"I once worked for the com-pany which came to be known as Shelter-corp and de-spite all this chaos it a-ppears they still have peo-ple work-ing for them." He went on to explain about his meeting with Mister Gaunt and the location he was instructed to attend in the town of Red-hill.

"I do not understand," said Angeline shaking her head. *"You clearly believe this to be lies, why are you going there? It all sounds rather ominous to me."*

The man took a few sips of water from a bottle and gave her a knowing look. "Angel-ine, you are not the only one, seek-ing ven-geance." The woman soon drifted off to sleep and was now lying against the slumbering Howler, who apparently didn't mind.

Spider had a lot on his mind and as he sat by the fireside, his thoughts returned to the days that followed his family's murder.

The first thing he was aware of was a faint rhythmic beeping of a heart monitor and with an effort he forced open his eyes. He felt different, colder somehow and his surroundings were strangely familiar. This was one of the trauma wards in the Los Demones general hospital. As a younger man he had worked in this place, but that now seemed like a lifetime ago. A nurse walked into the room and upon seeing he was awake, rushed away to find a doctor. A few minutes later, a short dumpy man wearing a doctor's coat arrived by his bedside with an armful of medical paperwork.

"Ah, Mister Hellstrom. I am pleased to say that you can expect to make a full recovery. It's been over a month since you were first admitted and to be honest none of us were ever sure you would wake up."

He glared at the man and turned to the window, where a black spider had just begun entwining an insect in its webbing.

The doctor wasn't paying attention to him and just continued to read through his medical notes. "Other than some minor scarring and a little facial hair loss from the fire, you are quite healthy."

The nurse turned on the television mounted on the wall and gave him the remote. The channel was muted, but what he saw on the screen made him want to scream in rage. He turned up the volume and listened as a group of reporters interviewed the multi-millionaire, oil-tycoon and senator, Robert Mosely about his new mega-mall that had just begun construction. The fat oaf wore a tight-fitting long black leather coat and was bragging about how many jobs he'd be providing to the good people of Los Demones. He went on to say how he'd soon be flying up to Canada for a conference to ensure his city a great deal on their gas. At that moment something inside of him snapped. Before the man knew what he was doing, he had climbed out of bed, changed into his tattered clothes and walked out of the hospital.

After making a few enquiries, he found himself at a graveyard, barely a mile from where he had lived. There on the marble tombstone at his feet, were the names of his beloved wife and children. Seeing their names carved into the rock somehow made things worse. All he could see in his mind were the terrible events that resulted in his family being taken from him.

A passer-by stopped next to him. "Doctor Hellstrom?"

"Do I know you?" he responded curtly.

"It's me, Harvey Trent, you performed the surgery that saved my life. I'm so sorry about what happened to your family."

He scowled at the man and whispered, "Your condolences are irr-elevant."

"Um, right," answered Harvey, slightly unnerved by the man's odd behaviour and lit a cigarette. "Do you want one?"

"I hear those things will kill you," stated the man coldly.

"I keep meaning to quit, here you take them," said Harvey thrusting the metal lighter and cigarette carton into his hands.

As he watched Harvey Trent timidly bustle away, he placed a cigarette between his lips and lit it. Everything had become clear to him. They were all flies waiting to be devoured and he was the spider which they all feared. The image of Robert Mosely's smug face loomed in his mind and he now knew what had to be done.

The winter winds blew bitterly cold that morning and as dawn's first light was cast over the airfield, a lone figure lay in wait. The white limousine he had been awaiting soon rolled into view and as the portly senator departed the car with his entourage, Spider moved ever closer. Mosely had three bodyguards with him, but none of them noticed the slender figure flitting between the shadows as they made their way to the hangar. Getting on board the private jet proved to be surprisingly easy and he crept into the galley unnoticed. The plane soon took to the air and it wasn't long before one of Mosely's men came looking for food in the galley. Spider had already shorted out the room's lights with the blade of his knife and watched unseen from the shadows as the obese man opened the metal door of the large refrigerator. The image of his children's blood-smeared faces once more preyed on his thoughts and with a snarl he kicked the appliance's open door, smashing it into the unsuspecting man. The startled bodyguard went to draw a pistol from his hip, but his action was intercepted with a single stab of a knife, leaving his bleeding gun-hand pinned to his waist. As the man tried to cry out, he found his attackers leather-gloved fist shoved in his open mouth. Spider forced his hand down the man's throat and observed with interest as the sweating man struggled for breath. A few moments later, Spider was calmly loading the corpse into the refrigerator. Watching from a gap in the galley doorway, he could see another of the guards heading in his direction, but the man veered off to enter the bathroom. The third guard seemed to be having an animated discussion with Mosely at the front of the plane and while no one was looking, he moved to the bathroom entrance.

The guard had neglected to lock the door behind him and he gently slid the door open. The heavily-built man was facing away from him, whilst whistling and urinating into the toilet bowl. There wasn't much room to manoeuvre in this tiny cubicle and Spider couldn't risk the guard having an opportunity to call out. Without hesitation he shoved the large man forward, slamming his head into the wall, grabbed hold of his neck and proceeded to force the stunned individual down to his knees. The man flailed his limbs wildly as Spider submerged his face below the yellow waters of the toilet bowl and held him there. A minute passed and the drowning man finally became still. Spider left him where he was and warily exited the bathroom. Using the tip of his knife, he turned the sign on the door lock to 'occupied' and whilst trying to remain unseen, approached the seating aisle. He was now positioned directly behind the rearmost seats, next to a rack of tethered luggage and the door of the plane. The third guard had clearly become suspicious regarding his colleague's prolonged absence and had now risen from his seat with his gun drawn. There was no cover to conceal his presence here and knowing he was about to be discovered, he looked about for a solution to his dilemma. Spider stood up in plain sight of the guard, with his hands raised in surrender.

"Who the fuck are you?" said the muscular dark-skinned man, while aiming his pistol at the unknown passenger. As the armed man moved closer to strike the stoic intruder, Spider grinned and pulled the plane's emergency door release. The door abruptly flew outwards, along with the remaining guard, whose terrified screams lingered as he was sucked from the plane, out into the open sky. Spider had tied himself to the luggage rack with one of the fastening belts and held on for dear life as the plane began to drastically lose altitude. The panicking Mosely had fallen from his seat and was lying in the aisle calling for help. Although the plane was still losing altitude, the air pressure in the cabin had begun to equalise and he took the opportunity to collect a parachute from under the nearest seat. Once he had strapped on the harness, he staggered over to the senator and dragged him to the exit. The man had no idea what was happening and thanked Spider profusely as he tied him to his parachute harness. The two men fell from the open hatchway and after plummeting hundreds of feet, Spider pulled the ripcord. As they drifted downwards through the clouds, Spider began to recognise where they were. The sight of the snow-capped Alaskan mountains loomed into view and now knowing they were many miles from civilisation, he smiled to himself. When they came to land, Spider deliberately shifted the weight of the impact to affect Mosely and as they crashed down into the snow, the man shrieked in pain.

"This way," said Spider, gesturing for the man to follow.

"Do you know where you're going?" asked the man as he limped after him. "Do I know you? Wait, were you the chef I ordered? I thought I cancelled your services?"

Spider said nothing and as they scaled the icy slopes, the gaunt figure suddenly stopped outside a cavern entrance.

"This will be ade-quate," said Spider.

"It sure will be nice to get out of these darn cold winds, but do you think the search teams will find us here?" asked Mosely looking to the grey skies above.

"Doubt-ful," replied Spider, as he unexpectedly struck the man over the head with hilt of his knife. Mosely fell onto his back in the cold snow and as he lost consciousness, he watched the stranger collecting a coil of rope from a bag.

When he awoke, Mosely found himself stripped of clothing and suspended from the roof of the ice cavern by ropes about his arms. "What the hell is going on!" yelled the man. "I demand whoever is responsible to release me immediately, I am an American Senator!"

Spider looked up from the fire burning beside him and picked up Vanja, "I know who you are, Sena-tor."

"Then let me go, or I'll see to it that you go to death-row!" blustered the ruddy-faced man.

Spider slowly paced around the hanging man and put on the senator's long black leather coat. "You are a mur-derer, Ro-bert Mose-ly and I am here to make you su-ffer."

"I've never killed anyone, this is a mistake!" screamed the man now shaking with both fear and the cold. As he took a moment to inspect his captor, a look of grim realisation crossed the man's face. "Oh God, you're that Hellstrom guy, but they said you were as good as dead!"

Spider suddenly leant in close to look him in the eye. "You and I are go-ing to have a ra-ther length-y con-ver-sation, but first I think I will have a meal". Spider grinned and held the gleaming blade of his knife to Mosely's face, "Did you know, some spe-cies of spi-der can survive for months by feed-ing upon a sin-gle kill?"

Each day, Spider would remove more flesh to eat from the whimpering senator and using his considerable medical expertise, he tied off the veins preventing his victim from bleeding to death.

The search and rescue teams eventually found them thirty-one days later, by which time the limbless and skeletal Mosely was beyond all hope of medical care. While Spider was taken to a maximum-security correctional facility to await trial, Robert Mosely died in agony before he ever reached a hospital.

Chapter Seventeen

"Divided We Fall"

When he heard the drone of engines and crazed laughter echoing down the tunnels, Spider didn't hesitate to wake the others.

"What is it?" mumbled Richard, still half-asleep, but then realised why his rest had been interrupted.

"That will be Carter and his friends," stated Angeline grimly.

Richard began to visibly panic, "Oh man, if they've got vehicles, how the hell are we gonna outrun them?"

After loading his shotgun, Spider tucked the firearm in his inside coat pocket and turned to Angeline. "Can your Howler carry more than one of us?"

The woman looked at Lily lying timidly beside her on the floor and ruffled the fur about her neck. *"I do not think she could carry all of us."*

Spider nodded in agreement. "Take Rich-ard with you to the town."

Angeline frowned. *"D'accord, but what about you?"*

Spider was puzzled by the woman's apparent concern for him, but replied, "I will join you la-ter... if I am a-ble."

The woman leant forward and kissed him on both cheeks. *"We will wait for you."* Spider smiled slightly at the woman's touch and strode out into the rail tunnel.

"We will wait for him?" commented Richard, looking somewhat incredulously at her.

"Mais oui, he is a brave man and I owe him my life," responded Angeline.

"Yeah, he's a real nice sociopathic torturing cannibal," muttered Richard sarcastically.

"People can change. Anyway we should go; I just hope Lily does not mind you being on her back," teased the woman whilst stroking the massive wolf's head.

Lily suddenly growled, causing him to hide behind the woman. "Why do I get the feeling I would've been better off staying with the sociopath!"

Angeline just rolled her eyes at the man and once they were back out in the tunnel she vaulted onto the Howler's back. The vehicle's droning engines were close now, but even with the threat of their imminent arrival, the petrified Richard still took several attempts to approach the huge animal, before finally climbing on to her back behind Angeline.

Concealed within the gloom of the tunnel, Spider watched his acquaintances desperately clinging to the charging beast's back as it disappeared into the blackness. He deduced they would have a fair chance of survival providing Lily did not tire before reaching the town. His apparent selfless choice to stay behind had been purely pragmatic. Now that he was alone, dealing with his pursuers would prove simpler. Judging by the multitude of approaching headlights, he had already determined their numbers would be too great to face directly. His goal now was to sufficiently deter them that they would abandon their chase. The fire he had set in the rear office was still burning fiercely and upon seeing the glare, the riders brought their bikes to a screeching halt. He heard one of the men yelling commands and observed with interest as two of the men reluctantly dismounted a quad bike to investigate the source of the light. Spider slipped back into the maintenance room, dashed down the short hallway to the illuminated office's entrance and reached into his holdall to retrieve something.

Barely a few seconds later, two shabby individuals walked gingerly through the maintenance doorway. Each of them was brandishing guns, but neither man looked to be particularly focused. They made a cursory sweep of the first small room and quickly moved on to approach the rear office. Both men stopped alongside the open door and seemed hesitant to enter.

"I ain't goin' in first, you can," whinged one of them in a nasal tone.

"Piss off, Nevil!" said the larger man, "Fine. I WILL go first, but I'm tellin' Razor you were bein' a chicken shit again!"

"Don't do that!" whined Nevil, while nervously fidgeting with the brim of his baseball cap. "He'll have me chopped up!"

"Tough shit," said the other man smirking and pushed past him to enter the fire-lit room.

Unknown to either man, Spider had been lying in wait behind the open door. In an instant the slender figure sprang from his hiding place to bring his open palm to collide with great force against the startled Nevil's throat, while simultaneously causing the office door to slam shut. The scrawny man choked, grasped at his neck and fell to the ground, wheezing for breath.

When his ally in the adjoining room heard the door close behind him, he immediately turned about to chastise his companion. "Stop fucking about, Nevil, there's no one in here!"

The door opened slightly to reveal a gaunt man, smoking a cigarette. "You are quite corr-ect, but there is some-one out here."

The large man raised his rifle to shoot, but hesitated when the stranger nonchalantly flicked the cigarette at him. "What's that meant to do? Singe me to death?" laughed the man. "You are so fucking dead!"

Spider stared down to between the man's feet and gave him a wicked grin, showing his discoloured yellow teeth. The baffled gunman glanced to the floor and as his gaze fell upon the puddle about his feet, he exclaimed, "What the fu—"

Spider closed the door just as the gasoline ignited and the screaming man was engulfed in scorching flame. The individual's pained cries brought a smile to his lips, but as he turned his attention back to Nevil, he found the scrawny man pointing a shotgun at his face.

From within the office they heard agonised screams followed by a loud boom.

"FOR FUCK'S SAKE!" growled Razor, as he dismounted his motorbike. "I told 'em not to fire guns down here. BOYS, spread out! We may be about to have ourselves some PARTY CRASHERS!"

Carter was surprised by the man's quick thinking. The roar of the motorcycles engines were bad enough, but that loud bang could well bring the Infected, or any other nasty critters lurking nearby running to find them. While most of his men spread out around the dank tunnel to keep watch, Razor and a few others entered the office to discern what had happened. They found Nevil standing over a skinny-looking corpse and clutching a leather coat he had just apparently scavenged from the body. The victim's entire face was missing and it wasn't difficult to ascertain why; wisps of smoke were rising from the shotgun held in Nevil's hand. When a few of the men congratulated the ugly wretch, he just shrugged, tugged the baseball cap down over his eyes and skulked back out into the lightless tunnels. The blaze in the adjacent room had now gone out and Razor walked over to inspect the blackened corpse, which he recognised as one of his party. He was pretty pissed off, although they had killed one of the guys they were looking for, they had lost one of their own in the process.

Carter wandered in and leant against the doorway, while eyeing the faceless corpse. "This one of our quarry?"

"Yeah, think that's the creepy guy with the knife," replied Razor whilst using one of his hatchets to sever a few chunks of charred meat from his former companion.

The old man looked back at the bare-chested corpse, "Did you find the knife on his body?"

"Dunno, maybe Nevil or one of the others took it," mused the smiling man, whilst enjoying dismembering the body. Before Carter could ask any more questions, the sound of gunfire reverberated outside in the rail tunnels.

"We've got Mite's burrowing in on us, boss!" blurted a breathless man as he rushed in to stand beside Razor and Carter. They all knew about the giant black termites that frequented the dark places throughout the city. 'Black Mites' as they called them, were enormous armoured ant-like insects, which were capable of spitting a corrosive slime dozens of feet. The worst part was, they could use their acid to burrow through earth and rock, so the huge pests could turn up almost anywhere.

When they stepped out into the rail passage, it became obvious to Carter that their predicament was dire. Looking about the tunnel, he could make out at least six of the hulking armoured insects locked in combat with the dozen or so remaining men and more of the creatures were crawling from various newly bored holes. Utterly unperturbed by the situation, Razor let out an insane laugh as he charged the nearest bug head-on with a hatchet raised in each hand. The crazed brute of a man hurled one of his axes into its head and as the Mite recoiled in pain, he fearlessly dived onto its back to repeatedly hack at its spine with his remaining hatchet.

Carter knew that despite Razor's fighting prowess, they would not survive this encounter unless the odds could be somehow tilted in their favour. He recalled Razor having mentioned that some of his boys were carrying dynamite and called out, "Re-group and use the explosives to seal those damn breaches!" The few men who heard Carter's cry immediately relayed the order to the others and the survivors quickly formed into small groups in an effort to stand their ground. While a majority of them worked together to fend off the insect's attacks, a few of them hung back in preparation to seal the new tunnels with dynamite.

One of the men was collecting explosives from a duffle-bag, when he spied a familiar figure trying to remain out of sight amidst the rail pillars. "Nevil, it's me Gerry. Come over here and give me a hand, you cowardly asshole!" The skulking individual, now wearing his newly acquired coat didn't reply, but walked briskly over to stand beside him. The only light down here was being cast from the motorcycle's headlights and he couldn't help but cringe at the sight of Nevil's illuminated face. Gerry had always considered the man to be rather repulsive, but in this light his features seemed oddly sagging and pallid. Between the clicking noises of the angry Mites and his comrade's distraught cries, who were being coated in the insect's burning spittle, he could barely concentrate.

"Nevil, help me light the fuses!" yelled Gerry, holding out several sticks of dynamite. He watched Nevil take out a metal lighter and much to his horror; he lit all the fuses at once. Before he could react, the slender man had raised a foot to his chest, kicked him backwards to collide with the other men and swiftly sprinted away.

A few seconds later the entire tunnel violently shook, as man and insect alike were torn asunder by the blast. Many of the groaning men who had been caught in the fringe of the explosion were suddenly silenced, as tons of rock and dirt descended to flood the passageway. In the wake of the explosion and the resulting cave-in, the tunnel was left seemingly devoid of life. As Carter crawled from the rubble, the fading roar of a single departing vehicle hung in the air. After a few minutes the dust began to settle and Carter found Razor trying to pull one of his men free from the vast heaps of stone, but his efforts only succeeded in ripping off the dying man's arm.

"Fuck! FUCK FUUUCK!" roared the enraged man, as he threw the bloody limb at one of the other survivors, causing them to topple over into the dirt.

Carter sympathised with Razor's anger; out of the sixteen men who had set out from the camp, only four of them were still alive and their vehicles had all been lost. Worse still, the way back to the city was now irrevocably blocked. He was certain he had heard one of the bikes drive away and as he walked a little further down the rail line, he perceived a ghostly face hanging in the darkness; placed upon an upright signal post before him, was the eyeless and limp flesh of Nevil's dead face.

Chapter Eighteen

"Going To Town"

They were relieved to see the glare of the midday sun shining brightly in the distance. It meant their frantic ride through the dank tunnels on the Howler's back was finally nearing its end. Oddly, there had been no sign of their pursuers, but just a few minutes previously they had heard the unmistakable sound of an explosion from somewhere down the line. Richard could see that Angeline was clearly concerned about those chasing them; she had repeatedly looked over her shoulder during their journey wearing a worried expression. A sudden thought occurred to him, was she actually worrying about Spider? Surely this attractive woman he was holding on to wasn't enamoured with that creepy lunatic? He dismissed the notion and tried to focus on the light ahead.

The passage grew rapidly wider as it intersected with other rail lines and a new problem presented itself. The tunnel's ceiling and walls were dripping with vast quantities of a familiar dull-glowing ooze. For many years the environment had been suffering repercussions from the worldwide nuclear and chemical related accidents caused by the first solar flare. The radioactive sludge that often gathered in the lower reaches of the cities had come to be known as 'Taint' and was a highly toxic substance consisting of a variety of deadly pollutants. A cluster of large bubbling lakes of Taint had formed on the ground before them, leaving little room to manoeuvre.

Angeline brought the panting Lily to a halt and looked back to Richard. *"We will have to go on foot from here I think."*

Richard carefully climbed down off the huge wolf's back to stand beside Angeline and took a few moments to stretch his aching limbs, before looking to the hazards ahead. "Hey, I don't know if Lily will be able to make it through here. We really don't want to get any of that shit on us!"

Angeline reached up to the Howler and gently stroked her nose. *"Lily, Ainsi!"* instructed the woman, whilst beckoning for the large animal to follow.

"Damn it, girl, I don't speak French," grumbled Richard. "What you saying?" Although he was having trouble comprehending her words, the Howler had apparently understood her perfectly and began to pace after the woman. While Angeline and Richard stuck to the narrow pathways to traverse the corrosive mire, Lily was left with no choice but to attempt a series of leaps to cross the expanses of volatile liquid. With the additional encouragement of Angeline's commands, the white-furred beast was soon reunited with them safely on the other side. Keen to be far from the radioactive Taint, they hurried out into the blinding light of day and as they squinted at the sun-drenched surroundings they became aware of the deathly silence.

The train station was completely devoid of the living or dead and as they climbed onto a nearby platform, they quickly discerned why. From this vantage point it was apparent that the lofty metal boundary fence that spanned the station was intact and although the main gates were open, they were completely blocked by dozens of abandoned vehicles. When Richard caught sight of what lay just beyond the gates, a chill ran down his spine. Towering atop dozens of long quivering fleshy-tentacles was a gigantic bulbous mass of bloody contorting viscera.

"What the hell is that thing?" whispered the wide-eyed man, who was now feeling very queasy.

"Mon Dieu!" replied Angeline as she too laid eyes upon the grotesque monstrosity. *"We need to get out of here!"*

At that moment a pack of roaming dogs dashed out from an alley into the street and upon sensing the animals, the repulsive being flung out several of its long slimy appendages. Only one of the seven feral dogs escaped, the others were ensnared by the tentacles and lifted to the pulsating mass of guts, where the yelping canines' bodies were slowly absorbed into its own flesh.

They stood in stunned silence, as they observed agonised faces of people and beasts stretched across the rippling surface of its deforming body.

"H-holy shit," stammered Richard. "Did that thing just take those dogs and merge with them?"

The sickened Angeline promptly doubled over and vomited over the concrete. She coughed, wiped the sick from her mouth and muttered, *"Surely that Infected thing did not used to be a person? It must have taken in a lot of bodies to have become so big!"* She looked to Lily, who let out a concerned whine as she lay flat on the platform in the shadow of the ticket office. Knowing there was no conceivable way for them to fight such a hideous creature, they began a fervent search for an alternative route to escape the rail yard.

The motorcycle's droning engine began to falter and after struggling on for a few more minutes, it stopped altogether. Spider squinted at the fuel gauge and was unsurprised to see the needle was pointing to empty. With the glare of the bike's headlights behind him, he continued down the pitch-black tunnel. He found himself wondering how his travelling companions were faring; they would be perhaps only an hour ahead of him, but now he was once more on foot, he would be unlikely to catch up with them.

After venturing blindly through the dark for what seemed like an age, he stumbled upon an open doorway situated to one side of the rail passage. It led to a vertical access shaft, which had a ladder running up the far wall. He paused at the base of the ladder and stared up at the faint light some distance above. The dull clank of his boots echoed loudly as he ascended the metal rungs and upon reaching the top, he found an iron hatch directly above him. The glow of daylight shone from its edges and after listening carefully for any signs of obvious danger, he flung the heavy hatch open. The sun was shining high in the cloudless sky and as he climbed from the dark shaft, the intense light left him momentarily blind. Having been in the perpetual darkness for so long, it took several minutes for his vision to adjust to his dazzling surroundings. It was likely early afternoon and he appeared to be standing on the corner of a quiet suburban street. Rows of townhouses with large lawns and white picket fences lined the roadside. On the sidewalk barely a dozen feet from him were two swollen grey-skinned corpses. After taking the opportunity to light a cigarette, he moved closer to inspect the cadavers.

The bodies looked to be heavily mutated and their heads seemed to be missing. Curiously the tissue joining at their necks had been torn and not cut as he had first assumed. The scene before him was strangely familiar and then it dawned upon him. Before he had departed the town of Shadowvale, the young boy, Michael had regaled him with some of the awful encounters he had endured during his journey. At the Fort Angel army base, he had met creatures much like these, which he had referred to as 'Bloats'. They had been survivors, who had been mutated by a bite from a giant parasitical insect. Worse still, as he once more inspected the ripped skin hanging loosely at the corpses necks, he recalled the boy telling him about the spider-like creatures that hatched from within the Bloat's skulls. Michael had called them 'Terrors' and had described them as fast-moving bony spiders, that attacked with multiple lashing tongues, before burrowing into their victim's skull. Reasoning that his reactions may prove insufficient to deal with a Terror, he retrieved the sawn-off shotgun from his coat pocket. With the firearm in hand, the man continued to smoke and walked his way down the middle of the sunlit street. Several Infected were shambling in the shadows of the surrounding houses, but he knew that while the daylight remained they would be reticent to leave their cover. A little further down the road he came across a curious sight; sat on the roof of a small general goods store were a fat man and a skinny woman, who appeared to be in a state of emotional distress. Spider watched unseen from behind a mailbox as the ruddy-faced man yelled abuse at the woman and struck her repeatedly about the head with the back of his hand. Spider had begun to walk away when the man spotted him.

"Hey, you!" shouted the man gruffly. "My wife and I need some help; there's something in the store below us. Get rid of it and I'll give you some of our food and drink!"

Spider stopped in his tracks, slowly turned around and shot the man a distrustful look. With the offer of much needed supplies, he reluctantly wandered back towards the general store. The main entrance was barricaded, but rather curiously the window at the building's rear had been propped open. He stepped onto the ledge and cautiously climbed through the wooden frame of the window.

Dropping silently to the dusty floor of a storeroom, he immediately heard a rasping noise from somewhere within the darkness of the adjoining room. While creeping towards the door, he could see the shop counter and several empty racks of shelving, but he still couldn't ascertain where the noise was coming from. With the shotgun held ready, he inched further into the gloom and just as he reached the counter, a loud inhuman hiss sounded from above. On instinct he threw himself sideways and a split-second later, a long-legged spider creature crashed down onto the floor where he had been standing. Its spindly long legs were bony and caused a rapid clicking as it rushed away back into the shadows.

The room once more fell silent and as Spider dared to move back to the door, a writhing mass of lengthy barbed-tongues suddenly coiled around his right leg. As he was pulled to the ground, he fired both barrels of the gun in the creature's direction, but inexplicably missed. The pain from his leg was excruciating and he could feel a swathe of blood running from the wound. The Terror began to drag him across the tiled floor and in desperation; he kicked out with his free leg to strike one of the towering shelving racks. The metal shelves rocked, before abruptly toppling to the floor with a loud crash, causing the parasite to wildly thrash about while emitting a high-pitched screech. The grotesque Terror's tongues had apparently become trapped beneath the weight of the rack and he could no longer feel them gripped about his leg. He limped over to the creature, reloaded the shotgun and took careful aim, before discharging the firearm. The Terror exploded into a pool of greenish slime, leaving only its many still-twitching legs. The rasping he had heard when first entering sounded once again from a nearby storage locker.

He drew Vanja and moved to open the locker, while poised to strike at whatever lay within. In one fluid motion he threw open the door and thrust the gleaming blade forward, but suddenly paused mid-strike. Sat within the cupboard was a trembling young blonde-haired girl, who looked up at him with dark tear-filled eyes. She initially looked terrified, but suddenly threw her arms around his waist and sobbed into his chest. Spider found himself cradling her head and looked down with confusion at her body. The girl was painfully thin and likely no more than eight years old. Her body and face were covered with dark bruises, while her arms bore dozens of small burn scars, which he knew had been caused by a lit cigarette.

Spider put away his knife and knelt down in front of her. "The crea-ture can-not hurt you now. What is your name?"

The child blinked back the tears welling in her brown eyes and meekly whispered, "Clara."

"I am Spi-" he began, but as he considered Clara's sad face, he replied, "You may call me Vîggo."

"My parents will be angry with me," said the scared girl, whilst holding her arms tightly to her chest and rocking from side to side.

"Why?" asked Spider calmly, as he rolled up a leg of his jeans to inspect the wound he had received.

Clara shuffled her feet nervously. "I was meant to get the food and drink for them, but I got scared and hid." Spider had just collected a bottle of whiskey from his holdall and winced as he poured some of the alcohol over the stinging lacerations to his leg. The room was suddenly flooded with daylight as a roof hatch was opened and Clara's parents peered down at them with grumpy faces. When they saw the Terror was dead, the two dour faced individuals descended to the shop floor using a rope ladder.

"Right, you can fuck off!" said the sneering man while pointing a rifle at Spider's chest. "And you can leave that bag of yours too!"

The scrawny woman nodded in agreement with her husband and turned to address her daughter. "As for you, you useless little bitch, you won't be getting any supper! And if you like hiding so much you can spend the night in that locker!" Spider scowled as the haggard woman shoved the crying girl inside the metal cabinet, slammed the door and locked it.

The husband poked him in the ribs with the barrel of the gun. "What you waiting for shit for brains? Toss your bag on the floor and get lost, or I'll put a bullet in your guts!"

Spider stared into the man's eyes and his lips formed into a small smile. "Go a-head, shoot."

"What?" responded the man slightly taken aback. "Look, you psycho, fuck off now, or you're a dead man!"

Spider leant forward against the gun now pressed to his stomach and snarled, "Do it." There was loud bang and Spider staggered backwards clutching his abdomen. As the smoke cleared, Clara's parents were shocked to see the tall figure standing up straight and holding up a vicious looking knife.

"Shoot him again, Bill!" shrieked the woman.

Bill was still staring in disbelief at the man's unblemished coat and as he raised the gun to fire again, Spider's mouth revealed a sinister grin, "I am go-ing to kill you, Bill."

The rotund man took one look at Spider's unblinking dark-ringed eyes and turned to run, but felt a searing pain in his trailing leg. He collapsed to the ground and stared in horror at the tip of a small knife blade protruding just below his knee. As Spider advanced upon the prone man, he heard the sound of breaking glass from beside him and the wife came screaming at him wielding a broken glass bottle. As the crazed woman reached him, he brought his open palm sweeping upwards to collide under her jaw with an audible crack. She fell in an undignified heap on the tiled floor and lay still. After yanking the throwing knife free from Bill's leg, he placed a foot on the injury and applied pressure, making the overweight man squeal in agony.

"I have chang-ed my mind," said Spider. "Stand up." The groaning man did as he was told and as he slowly climbed back to his feet, Spider slashed Vanja's razor edge horizontally across the expanse of his fat belly. The bleeding man staggered backwards as his slippery innards tried to slide out from the gaping tear.

"Here, let me help you," said Spider, as he grabbed the man's hands and pushed them to his sliced stomach. He opened the store's front door and escorted the petrified Bill to the doorway. "I be-lieve it is time for you to leave."

"But I'll die out there," wheezed Bill, while struggling to contain his guts within his belly.

Spider grinned and held up his knife to the man's right eye. "I am cer-tain I can keep you a-live for many hours if you would prefer?"

Bill limped from the store as fast as he could, leaving a heavy trail of blood behind him. The sun was beginning to set and Spider knew the nearby lurking Infected would devour him within the hour. He unlocked the door of the metal locker, picked up the shaking Clara and placed her to sit on the shop counter. She watched with mixed feelings as the tall stranger bundled her unconscious mother into the cabinet and locked the door.

Spider turned to look at her. "Two more mon-sters that will not be hurt-ing you any-more".

Clara nodded. "I don't think I will miss them". The young girl looked at her father's blood coating the tiled floor and asked, "Are you a bad man?"

Spider shrugged. "Some-times."

Chapter Nineteen

"A Good Man"

They spent the night in the storeroom, from where they could barely hear Clara's mother's incessant demands to be free from the cabinet. Several of the hungry Infected outside on the street were drawn by her cries, but thankfully the night passed without further incident. In the morning Clara presented Spider with a large rucksack brimming with food and drink, which she had collected from under the shop counter. As they ate their breakfast, he watched Clara pick out a few comic books from a stand by the cash register. A science related magazine stood out amongst the other publications and he picked it up to browse the pages. He was amazed to find one of the articles concerned an experimental molecular-altering substance called 'Diamondinium', which could make steel, virtually unbreakable. After taking out the vial he had procured from the safe at the survivor camp, he drew Vanja from his coat pocket and pondered the curious substance. While Clara was giggling at the antics of cartoon characters, he poured the glowing blue liquid into a glass beaker he had found on one of the store's shelves and with some hesitation, dropped Vanja point-first into the Diamondinium. The liquid frothed and bubbled as it reacted to the immersed metal blade. When Spider saw the hilt's leather bindings dissolve, he became somewhat alarmed and reached out to snatch the knife from the steaming beaker, but decided to wait a little longer. His patience appeared to pay off and the liquid began to quickly evaporate, until finally all that remained was his grandmother's unblemished hunting knife. Despite the loss of the leather grip, the familiar weapon felt much the same in his hand, but its keen edge somehow seemed even sharper than before. If that news article was accurate, Vanja was now composed of a super-dense alloy, allegedly capable of piercing almost any known material.

"What you doing?" asked the small girl, peering up at the steaming glassware on the counter.

"A li-ttle chem-istry," replied the man absent-mindedly while still examining the blade.

"Cool," said Clara seemingly accepting his answer at face value. "Will we be going somewhere today, Vîggo?"

Spider cast her a puzzled look. "You will not want to go where I am head-ing. Is there some-where safe I can take you?"

Clara bit her lip as she contemplated his question. "My teacher, Mrs Linney was real nice and she lives at the school. I don't think it's very far from here. She was really pregnant, so I think she would have stayed there."

"Ve-ry well," answered Spider with a fleeting smile, "You had better show me where this place is."

When they stepped out onto the street they found the weather drastically changed from the previous day's sunny climes. Stinging black rain pelted down from the tempestuous skies overhead, to sizzle in puddles on the asphalt and as the two of them dashed through the cascades of burning liquid, they soon sought shelter from the searing rains. Spider could see a residence with a large wooden porch up ahead and without thinking, he scooped up the weary child in his arms, before sprinting to the house. On the deck of the porch was a body of an old man slumped forward in a rocking chair and as they reached the cover of the veranda, the figure lifted its rotting head to view them with bleeding eyes. They had both spotted the Infected rising from the chair and Clara let out a little fearful gasp as Spider promptly lowered her to the ground. The foul-smelling creature hungrily snapped its jaws open and shut as it lurched towards the frightened little girl, but found another blocking its path. Spider snarled as he dashed forward to slash Vanja across the sagging flesh of its neck. Blood sprayed across the decking as the immense blow sheared its decaying head from its shoulders, which then bounced down the wooden steps into the waterlogged road.

The soaking wet girl shuddered as she eyed the headless body lying at her feet. "I think my school is just on the other side of this house." The man paused to marvel at his deadly handiwork, before giving her a nod and easing the open the front door. Within the dusty hallway, they found the bodies of two women hanging from lengths of rope coiled about their necks.

Spider had come across many suicide victims during his travels and was unfazed by the swinging corpses, but found himself instinctively shielding Clara as they walked past them. One of the bodies suddenly began to thrash about and groan, but Spider just hurried the startled Clara out through the back door.

Outside, the rains had grown heavier and the sky had darkened so greatly that it appeared to be night. On the opposite side of the street they could now see Clara's school and there appeared to be large 'Help!' signs pressed to the inside of the upper floor's windows. Spider took the small girl by the hand and splashed through the stinging rains of the chemical storm. Upon reaching the cover of the main entrance's balcony, the soaked couple leant against the school doors to catch their breath.

"This is the place, Vîggo," sighed Clara.

"What is wrong?" asked Spider confused by the sadness in her small voice.

"Mrs Linney is nice, but—" her voice trailed off mid-sentence.

Spider frowned. "But what?"

"I think I'd be safer with you." Before he could respond, she had thrown her arms about him in a tight embrace him and whispered, "Please don't leave me."

While staring up at the foreboding clouds in the sky, the man swept back his short blond hair with both hands, wiping the rain from his head. "I have al-ready told you it would not be safe to stay with me. Now, let us find your teach-er." The small girl initially pouted, but then quietly placed her hand in his, and with some apprehension the two of them wandered inside.

They had resorted to stacking several wooden crates against the train station's high fence to escape the compound and upon fleeing the area, they had ended up spending the night in the back of a heavy goods trailer on the highway. The sun had risen, but the sky remained dark outside and it was now pouring down with rain.

"Morning," said Richard glumly, as he passed Angeline some of their remaining water. "Doesn't look like that 'Taker' followed us at least."

"Magnifique," replied the woman, as she poured out some of the liquid into a pan for the dozing Howler to drink. *"You mentioned before that you intended to go your own way, do you have any plans?"*

Richard pursed his lips and retrieved a crumpled photograph from his shirt pocket. "That's my wife and son," said the man while showing her the picture. "They 'were' my plans. Guess all I can do now is try to find a safe place to live out my days."

"Ah, I see," said the woman, while stroking Lily's head. *"Spider told me where he was headed and I intend to help him."*

"Really?" replied Richard in an incredulous tone. "Please tell me you don't have feelings for that nut job!"

Angeline stood up and glared at him. *"That 'nut job' has saved both of our lives more than once and I know he has some serious problems, but I believe he is a good man. As for my personal feelings, they are none of your business!"* She then tapped the Howler on the nose to wake her and stormed out of the trailer. After collecting a large parasol lying at the side of the road, she climbed onto the huge wolf's back and opened the umbrella to shield her and Lily from the rain.

Richard followed her out into the grim weather a minute later. "Look, I'm sorry for what I said, but I will be taking the first working vehicle I find out of this place."

"Fine," said the woman and they continued down the road together in abject silence.

After spending all those days trekking through the desolate ruins of City-6, Angeline found it strange to see the rows of untouched houses standing all around her.

"I don't believe it!" yelled Richard excitedly. He pointed to a dented pickup truck abandoned on the overpass directly ahead, "That's my truck!"

Angeline squinted at the vehicle in the distance and asked, *"What is that strange yellow blob in the driver seat?"*

Richard wasn't listening and was already jogging through the rain to his truck. Slumped at the wheel was Clarence's body, still dressed in the plastic hazmat suit, which was oddly dripping with Taint.

"Damn!" exclaimed the man. "My ride's full of that glowing shit!"

Angeline watched with dismay as the yellow suited body rose from the seat and staggered to approach the distracted Richard, who was busy checking something on the vehicle's trailer. As she spurred Lily to race them to his aid, she saw the man raise a pistol at the 'Tainted' figure.

"You really don't look too good, Clarence!" babbled Richard nervously while backing away from the oozing being. He fired all six rounds in the chamber of his revolver and although each scored a hit, they just punctured neat holes in the suit, from which more viscous Taint poured out. The terrified man ran back towards his companion who had just arrived astride the huge wolf. "Bullets don't work, run!"

Angeline slid from atop the beast to the ground and took out something from her rucksack. There was a sudden loud sizzling as the flare soared from her gun to impact on the chest of the Tainted and the being was immediately enveloped in fierce flames.

Richard's mouth fell agape as the burning figure suddenly burst apart into a giant pool of glowing slime, leaving virtually no trace of the former man's body. "What the fuck?"

"Search and rescue," said the bemused woman, while smiling at the flare gun in her hand.

She looked on with sadness as Richard mounted the motorbike that had been lashed to the pickup's trailer. *"You are really leaving?"*

"I'm sorry. I just need to be alone. Oh, if you find Spider, please don't tell him I took his bike!"

Angeline smiled and kissed him on both cheeks, before once more climbing onto Lily's back. As the man rode down the highway and disappeared over the horizon, she whispered, *"Au revoir, Richard. I truly hope you find what you are looking for."*

"Carter! Think I've just FOUND us our dinner!" laughed Razor, as he pried open the storage locker to stare at the skinny woman, who had been calling out for help.

"All in good time, let's see if the bitch knows anything," replied the old man standing in the store doorway. The hysterical woman willingly told them about the stranger in the leather coat and what he'd done to her beloved husband. She went on to explain that she had heard that man and her evil daughter discussing going to a nearby school.

The very moment she had nothing useful left to say, the muscular individual dismembered her with his hatchets into multiple pieces. The blood covered man chuckled to himself, "HEY, Carter! People were always telling me I should go BACK to school!"

Chapter Twenty

"A Bitter Reunion"

The rain pattered heavily against the tall windows that lined one side of the corridor and as they moved past the water-smeared glass, there was a flash of intense light, followed by an almighty crash of thunder. The sudden bright light and noise caused the small girl to cling hold of Spider out of fright.

The man placed a hand on her shoulder and gestured to the street outside. "The storm will soon pass."

"I thought it was another one of those solar flares," answered Clara meekly.

"Un-like-ly," replied the man, as he lit a cigarette. Clara tugged on his arm and pointed to a 'No smoking' sign on the wall. Spider rolled his eyes dismissively and turned his attention to a 'Save the children' charity poster on a nearby notice board. The first word had been changed with a black marker to read 'Kill'.

"Plea-sant school you have here," remarked Spider.

"Don't think it said that before," said Clara moodily, who was now frowning at the smoking man in disapproval, with her arms crossed across her chest. There was another lightning flash and for a second Spider thought he could make out a dark twisted shape standing at the end of the hallway. While remaining perfectly still, he held Clara with one hand and drew his knife with the other, but when the next flash illuminated the corridor, there was nothing there.

"What's wrong?" whispered Clara, as she stared at the same dark space beyond the entrance hall.

Spider's eyes narrowed as he took another drag of his cigarette. "Per-haps noth-ing. Show me where your teach-er lived." Clara led him along the halls to the rear of the school, to a door marked: 'Mrs Joyce Linney – Headmistress'.

She raised a hand to knock on the door, but hesitated and looked to Spider. "We were told not to disturb her out of school hours, unless it was important."

The man gave her a knowing look, "Con-sider-ing the glo-bal catas-trophe, I think we can a-ssume it is an e-mergen-cy."

Clara bobbed her head in agreement and knocked on the wooden door causing it to swing open wide. "Sorry! I didn't mean to break it!" blurted the little girl, while flinching in expectation of being punished.

He took the smouldering cigarette stub from his lips and extinguished it on the door frame. "I have no inten-tion of hurt-ing you, Clara. I think we should take a look in-side. Stay close to me." The relieved girl quietly nodded and followed him through the doorway. Shards of a broken mirror, which had been hung over a fireplace, lay strewn about the carpeted floor. Amidst the pieces of jagged glass, were strange patches of reddish slime, which appeared to be smeared over almost every surface. Not wanting to linger in this place, he pushed open the bathroom and bedroom doors, but there was no one present in either room. He paused in the bedroom doorway, the quilt of the double bed was rolled back to reveal blood drenched sheets.

"We need to leave," said Spider with some urgency, whilst backing out of the room.

"But, where is Mrs Linney?" asked Clara trying not to cry. Spider didn't reply and as they left the woman's apartment, an abrupt blood-curdling scream echoed from somewhere down the hall. Taking Clara by the hand, Spider raced back to the main entrance, but found the way blocked. Before them, bent over an eviscerated man's body, was a huge, misshapen, naked female form. Her features were grossly deformed and an abundance of blood was trickling from her red eyes. The gurgling being caressed its swollen stomach as its jaws tore into the flesh of the dead janitor's guts.

Spider started to edge away, pulling Clara with him, but the small girl burst into tears and called out, "Mrs Linney?" The Infected creature hissed as it noticed their presence and moved to advance upon them, but unexpectedly stopped. Just as the Infected began to screech in apparent pain, Spider picked up Clara, turned, and ran.

Looking back over the man's shoulder, Clara winced in horror as a rasping fleshy mass slipped out from between the mutated teacher's legs, to crawl along the tiled floor.

"Vîggo, she had a baby!" shrieked the girl hysterically. As the man sprinted down the corridor carrying the distraught child, several more of the Mother's 'Children', crawled from the shadows to converge upon them. Spider skidded to a halt, rushed into a nearby classroom and slammed the door, before quickly barricading the entrance with several desks. The moment the door was shut, they heard the fervent scraping of small fingers scratching at the base of the door, before it suddenly fell eerily silent.

"Have they gone?" murmured Clara softly, still trembling with fear. Spider held up the index finger of a gloved hand to his lips, gesturing for her to be quiet.

She wanted to ask what he was listening for, but then became aware of the creaking of metal from above. "They're in the vents!" exclaimed the girl, staring worriedly up at the ceiling.

Spider was considering the merits of attempting to leave via the way they came in, when a succession of heavy blows struck the door, rattling the desks piled in front of it.

"It a-ppears Moth-er is look-ing for us," commented the man dryly, while scouring the classroom for an alternate exit.

He rushed over to the windows, but cursed silently when he found metal bars fixed to the outside. Knowing that the Mother or its Children could break into the room at any second, he loaded the remaining shell into the shotgun and fired it at what he hoped was an inner wall. The resulting blast caused a cloud of plaster to fill the air and just as the Mother smashed its way into the classroom, he charged at the weakened partition with the young girl in his arms.

They crashed through the dusty plaster and tumbled awkwardly onto a wooden stage, surrounded by musical instruments. Hearing the lumbering approach of the Infected being, he scrambled to stand and swiftly hauled Clara to her feet. Seeing the Mother was reaching through the hole to grab the startled girl, Spider took hold of a cello by its neck and swung the hefty instrument into the vile creature's face. The impact caused a large portion of its sallow features to burst open in a spray of blood and yellow oozing pus. While the Infected recoiled from the attack, Clara ran across the stage to some heavy looking curtains. She pulled back the drapes and heaved on the fire exit doors, but found they wouldn't budge. As Spider dashed over to join her, he could now see the problem; the doors were secured by a bulky metal padlock and chain. On the other side of the room, the Mother was furiously tearing at the breach in the wall, in a bid to reach them.

Spider went to retrieve Vanja from his pocket, but was confused to find it missing and muttered, "Where is my knife?"

"I can see it!" said Clara, and before he could reply, she was racing back across the stage to where they had fallen. He turned to chase after her, but found two of the Mother's hissing offspring crawling at his feet. Their appearance resembled that of a newborn child, but their slimy skin was almost translucent and covered with bulbous bloody veins, while their hungry mouths held full sets of gnashing teeth. With a running kick, he punted one through the air, to squelch against the far wall. The remaining infant clasped its wiry arms about his shin in an effort to bite him, but the man ripped it free with both hands and hurled it to the floor with contempt. There was a loud crunch as he brought a foot stamping down on the writhing creature, bursting its rotten innards across the wood floor, and then he heard a shrill cry for help. Looking up, he could see the Mother had pulled its bloated frame halfway through the enlarged hole and with its one free arm, had caught hold of Clara's leg. The crying girl was being swiftly dragged backwards on her belly towards the rasping monstrosity and in moments would be devoured. Spider sprinted across the room, but already knew it was too late.

Clara shrieked as the Infected's leathery arm pulled her beneath the sagging flesh of its body and dropped its head down to feed. As the Mother's open mouth snapped forward to tear into the young girl's flesh, there was a horrific sound of crunching bone. Spider growled in frustration and crushed another of the loathsome crawling children beneath his boot. A faint sobbing began to emanate from the oddly-still Mother. He walked over to investigate and was shocked to discover one of Clara's arms frantically flailing from beneath the stinking mass of rotting flesh. Taking hold of the girl's limb with both hands, he hauled her free, to find she was surprisingly unharmed.

"I do not under-stand," remarked Spider, as he helped her up from the floor. The little girl was still visibly shaken, but pointed at the head of the dead creature; protruding from top of its skull was Vanja's hilt. Seemingly by luck, she had managed to ram the vicious blade into the foul monster's brain. After collecting his knife, he escorted the traumatised girl to the fire exit. He forced Vanja's point into the padlock's keyhole and just as he had hoped, the augmented blade cut into the steel, breaking the lock. Pulling the chain from the door, he kicked open the fire exit and walked out into the stinging rain beside Clara.

The fire exit led out into a narrow alley between two high-walled buildings and although the rains burned their skin, it was good to be away from the stench of the Infected. As they made their way along the alley, several very large rodents, often referred to as Vermin, scurried away from the open dumpsters.

"Will you be looking after me now?" asked Clara, gazing up at him with tearful brown eyes.

He sighed. Logic dictated he should just walk away, but the idea once more conjured up the painful memory of his children's dead faces. He crouched down beside her to look her in the eye. "I am not a good man, Clara".

"Yes, you are!" argued the pouting girl, while stamping her feet and wiping away her tears.

Spider shook his head. "You do not under-stand. I am not the man, I once was."

"Please don't leave me, Vîggo," implored Clara, as she leant against his shoulder.

"Well, well. Ain't this touching!" said a brusque voice from behind. Spider immediately stood up and turned to face two figures standing barely a dozen feet from him. The larger of the two men, looked crazed and was wielding two hefty hatchets. The older grey-haired man, who had just spoken, had drawn two pistols from his belt and appeared to be smiling.

The moment Spider had heard the voice he had sequestered his throwing knife to be hidden within his palm. As the two men stepped closer, he held Clara behind him, he had no doubt they would gun her down the moment she tried to run. "You must be Cart-er," said Spider scowling.

The old man smirked. "That's right, boy. I'm sure Angeline told you all about me, so where is that French whore? Anyhow, I reckon you're the guy who took down my crew at the farm."

As Carter stepped from the shadows, Spider stared at his face with perceptible hatred and snarled, "You..."

The old man paused in his tracks as he inspected the glowering man. "Do I know you, boy?"

"You kill-ed my fam-ily," whispered Spider coldly.

"WHAT the FUCK is going on?" yelled Razor. "Are we KILLING this chump or what?"

Carter laughed. "I don't fucking believe it! I did some work for a guy named Mosely some years back, and I could have sworn I torched this asshole in Los-Demones. Seem to remember your lady and kids screamed real loud before they died!"

Before another word could be spoken, Clara screamed in horror. As a shadow fell across the alley, they all looked up at what had frightened the little girl. Towering above them, atop a multitude of lengthy fleshy-tentacles, was a gigantic throbbing mass of bloody flesh. Despite knowing he could be killed by the gargantuan Infected at any moment, Spider went to throw the knife at Carter's throat, but upon hearing Clara's terrified cries, he picked her up and fled into the street. The ground shook as a swarm of large Vermin scampering behind him were suddenly swept up in a throng of pulsing tentacles. The Infected being pulled the squirming rodents up to its bulbous body, where the squeaking beasts were irrevocably merged into its quivering flesh. Spider could see several crashed vehicles were blocking the road ahead, without slowing his frantic pace he leapt onto the hood of a car and ran onwards, just as another host of giant tendrils slammed down onto the road to ensnare them. The enormous grotesque being let out a deafening wail as it lashed out yet more of its appendages in a frenzy to catch them. Its tentacles smashed into the adjacent townhouses, bringing the buildings crashing down all around them. As a seemingly endless barrage of bricks and debris rained down, Spider threw himself head first through a broken store window.

Razor laughed uncontrollably as the fleshy coils took hold of him, and as the Taker lifted him up to join its body, he took out something from his pocket.

After lighting the fuses with a lighter, he held the dynamite aloft and yelled, "Here comes your PRESENT!" The crazed man continued to laugh until there was a sudden ear-splitting boom. While gallons of bloody gore cascaded down from the creature's craterous wound to splatter over the streets below, the massive Infected staggered back and forth for several seconds, before finally toppling to the ground with a mighty crash.

Carter climbed out of the dumpster and surveyed the carnage covering the street with a quiet calm. As he turned to exit the alley, he was startled to find a tall man dressed in a smart suit, blocking his path. The almost-skeletal figure had ice-like skin and the pupils of his eyes were shining white. "Where the hell did you come from?"

The well-attired man adjusted his black tie and smiled. "A pleasure to meet you, Mister Carter. My employers have instructed me to make you a rather lucrative proposition."

The old man listened to the stranger's offer with great interest and his mouth formed into a wicked grin; he had taken that Swedish man's loved ones away once, now he would do it again.

Chapter Twenty-One

"Ultimatum"

The young girl knelt beside the unconscious figure and whispered, "Please wake up, Vîggo."

The man had sustained a nasty gash to his temple during his fall through the pet store window and Clara began to search the shelves for something to help him. She found a padded dog basket behind the counter and used it as a pillow to prop up his head. After collecting the bottle of alcohol from the man's holdall, she soaked a piece of cloth in the pungent liquid and dabbed the cut, much as she had seen him do to his leg wounds when they had first met. It was still raining outside and the sun was starting to go down. Although the seven year old didn't miss her abusive parents, Clara desperately wished she wasn't alone right now. With great effort she managed to drag a shelf unit in front of the broken window, so anything wandering by wouldn't see them. She then sat back down beside the agitated looking Vîggo, who was muttering in his sleep. Unknown to Clara, Spider was reliving a dark period from his past.

The trial did not go as he expected. Despite being found guilty of murder by a unanimous jury, the judge ruled that due to the mitigating circumstances of the tragic loss of his family, and the fact he had saved so many lives during his medical career, that he would not bestow the death sentence. Within the day he was transferred to the Blackvine sanatorium, located on the outskirts of Los Demones. The judge declared that he would spend the rest of his days at that maximum security asylum, without possibility of parole. Over the next few months, Spider, as he now called himself, preyed upon the other inmates, brutally torturing them, before consuming their flesh. Ultimately the facility's personnel were forced to keep him in solitary confinement, and from then on he was only allowed to leave his cell while accompanied by Taser-wielding orderlies.

It was an early afternoon in August and two burly orderlies had just arrived to release him for his daily exercise in the yard. As they escorted him down the sunlit sterile corridor to the yard entrance, there was a blinding flash and the whole sky seemed to be suddenly filled with fire. While the orderlies froze in panic, Spider dropped on instinct to the concrete; in mere moments the exposed men's flesh began to burn and shrivel. The unmistakable odour of cooking meat flooded the air and when the temperature finally diminished, the staff members cowering forms were left as smoking blackened husks. Many of the thick glass windows that lined the hall had shattered in the intense heat and Spider smiled slightly as he picked up a jagged shard of glass from the warm stone floor. As screams and inhuman cries echoed from around the complex, he calmly walked back towards the dining hall. He was intrigued to find several patients and staff members convulsing on the ground, while others were desperately trying to defend themselves from a number of hissing grey-skinned creatures, with drooling split jaws.

Many of the quivering figures lying around him began to transform into more of the abhorrent milky-eyed beings. Undeterred, Spider strode forward brandishing his makeshift shiv and begun to instinctively puncture the vital organs of the mutants. His actions on that day tilted the tide of battle and inadvertently saved several lives.

A few days later, when the asylum was once more under control, he received an unexpected visitor. Spider was shown into a small interview room, where a well-dressed young man was sat at the far side of a table, viewing some paperwork.

"Please, take a seat, Mister Hellstrom," said the man while still reading through the documents. Spider sat down opposite him and lay back in his seat showing a disinterested glazed expression.

"I'm sorry to inform you that your cannibalistic tendencies have caused you to develop a progressive neurodegenerative condition, otherwise known as a prion disease."

Spider knew that such illnesses often caused severe deterioration to the mental processes of the brain and the subject's physical motor functions. Oddly, he felt fine.

The man sat opposite him continued, "However, I have 'some' good news. It appears your immune system has inexplicably prevented any major damage from your prion related condition. Also, despite receiving bites during the recent mutant pandemic, you appear to be showing no sign of infection from the 'Grey-Maw' disease."

Spider was no longer listening and was tightly rolling up the medical documents, while considering whether he could force the papers down the man's throat before the orderlies outside could stop him.

Oblivious to Spider's murderous intentions, the man then smiled. "Well, I may also have some other news for you. As you may have heard, the UN government are setting up a new organisation to counter future global threats. It's being called the Shelter-Corp initiative and due to your considerable medical expertise, they have shown an unexpected interest in you. Mister Hellstrom, it seems they wish to offer you a research position at one of their facilities."

For the next few hours Clara sat quietly in the darkness, waiting for Vîggo to awaken. The girl soon found herself almost as bored as she was scared and got up to take a peek in the back room. Amidst the tall metal racks, filled with various animal related goods, was a wheezing body trapped beneath a fallen stack of shelves. The store owner had clearly become one of the decaying Infected and gurgled as it reached out towards her. Clara made sure to keep away from the disgusting thing and edged around the room to look at some of the large packages stacked against the back wall.

After some deliberation, she decided to open the boxes. Amongst the cans of pet food and bags of kitty litter, she found a white plastic, domed object with several tool-like arms. It was heavy, but with an exerted effort, Clara lowered it to the floor to take a better look at it. It stood about two feet high and had a metal stamp on its front that read: 'Automatech'. She pressed the power button on top of the dome, but it just caused a little red battery light to begin flashing on and off. Disappointed, the girl returned to Vîggo's side and lay down to get some rest.

Angeline and Lily were nearing the address now, but as they raced through the stormy night, the large wolf kept pulling them in a different direction. She had not known Lily to react like this before and decided to see where she wanted to go.

"Lead on then, Lily." When the beast realised she was no longer being directed, she bounded down a side street, covered with chunks of slime-covered meat. The woman didn't like the look of the fleshy debris on the road and dearly hoped Lily had not pulled them here just to eat the gruesome looking entrails. She was quite amused however, when the animal stopped to poke her head through a pet store's broken window

"D'accord, Lily. I will go in and have a look for you," said the woman as she dismounted. *"Perhaps I will find you some pet shampoo."* The white-furred Howler seemed to dislike this idea; she grizzled and lay flat on the sidewalk.

Angeline screwed up her face as she caught a whiff of her own scent in the wind. *"Oh dear, I think I need a bath too!"*

Finding the store entrance was locked solid; she carefully climbed through the hole in the window. As she eased herself onto the shop floor, she was taken-aback to see Spider and a little blonde-haired girl asleep in the corner of the room. Crouching down next to Spider, she became aware of a deep cut on his forehead. She gently shook him, but couldn't seem to rouse the man.

"Who are you?" cried the startled little girl, who had just risen to her feet.

"I'm Angeline," said the woman smiling and then gestured to Spider. *"This is my friend."*

Clara relaxed a little. "My name is Clara Mason, how did you find us?"

"Ah, I have my furry friend to thank for that," said Angeline. *"Lily, is still outside, as she could not fit through that hole."* Upon hearing her name, the massive wolf poked her head through the window, causing Clara to flee behind the counter.

"Do not be scared, she will not hurt you," whispered Angeline. After a few minutes of encouragement, Clara petted Lily's head and subsequently the little girl seemed a lot more at ease with the animal's presence. Angeline managed to open the store door from the inside and Lily padded in from the rain to lie down next to them. Once they had found some dog food on the shelves for the Howler to eat, Clara proceeded to share some supplies with the woman. As they ate their meal, the two of them swapped stories and after an hour of chatting, they settled down to get some sleep.

From across the street, the grey-haired man watched with delight as the French woman arrived astride a large white beast. He hadn't expected her to make this job so easy. Upon inspecting the tranquiliser pistol he had been given, he wondered whether the drug would prove to be effective on the woman's animal. After waiting a while, he loaded the ammo cartridge into the gun and approached the store. He was annoyed to find there was no line of sight to his targets from the shop's exterior. Stealth would likely not help him here, as the beast may have already caught his scent. Without further hesitation, he burst through the window and immediately turned the gun on the Howler. As Lily went to pounce upon the intruder, the man fired three darts into the animal's flank, making her yelp and then flop helplessly onto her side. Angeline stood up and went to draw her flare gun, but felt the sting of two darts in her chest and promptly collapsed. Clara was too scared to move, but Carter fired a shot in her back regardless. He looked down at the unconscious man and smiled. It would be so easy to kill him right now, but that was no longer the plan. Opening the store's door, he proceeded to drag the two females to his newly acquired jeep. The arrangement he had made with that stranger seemed to be working out well for him, although he still didn't understand why they didn't want him to simply bring the man to them. After tying up the captives, he returned to the store to drop an envelope on Spider's body. On the way out through the door, he couldn't resist firing a few rounds from his revolver into the sleeping Howler. Watching the lake of blood pooling around the white-furred animal brought a satisfied smile to his face. He then got back into his vehicle and set off towards the agreed rendezvous point.

With a sudden intake of breath, he shocked himself awake, and held his throbbing head as he shakily stood up. Daylight was shining through the open door and an envelope had just fallen from his chest, to the dusty floor. His head was spinning and his vision was blurred. Where was Clara? Leaning against the wall to steady himself, he was confused to find Lily lying in a puddle of blood beside him. The Howler's breathing was laboured and her tongue hung limply from the side of her open salivating jaws. Spider could see three neat blood-weeping holes in the beast's abdomen, clearly made by gunshots. Without the necessary medical supplies needed to save her, logic dictated he should put the creature out of its misery, but he found he didn't want to end her life needlessly.

Picking up the envelope, he could see the Shelter-Corp logo printed on one side and his name on the other. There was a small note inside which read; 'We have your wife. We have your friends'.

Dropping the note in disgust, he wandered into the back room to survey the shelves. A partially crushed Infected grabbed at him as he walked past, but Spider nonchalantly stabbed Vanja into its rotten skull and yanked the blade free, before continuing his search. He sighed; there wasn't anything here to treat the beast's injuries. All he could find on the racks were parasite treatments and vitamin supplements. There was an odd beep noise from the back of the room, followed by a mechanical whirring as a white robot with three blue glowing eye-stalks trundled forward on its tracks.

"Hi there, buddy!" said the automaton in a cheery nasal American accent. "Are you like, my owner?" Spider ignored the robot and wandered back out to end Lily's suffering.

"Oh, gee," said the machine in an overly sad tone. "Guess this Medi-bot doesn't have an owner!"

The man stopped in the doorway and turned around. "Medi-bot?"

"Yes-sir! That's me!" replied the robot cheerfully. "Although my manual says this unit is called Eddie. Eddie the Medi-bot! Hey, that kind of rhymes!"

Spider ignored the automaton's annoying banter. "There is an ani-mal in the next room that re-quires your attention."

"Whoa! Hold your horses, feller!" said the Medi-bot sternly. "Only my owner can tell me to do stuff!"

He rolled his eyes and sighed. "Fine. I am your ow-ner. Now, a-ssist the beast in that room."

The machine excitedly span about in a circle, while waving its tool arms erratically. "Nice to meet you, sir! My facial recognition software has now logged you as my legitimate owner!"

Spider stood in silence waiting for the robot to do something. "Well?"

"Well, what?" replied the Medi-bot absent-mindedly. "Oh, right! The animal! Oopsie!" Spider watched as the automaton raised its height using hydraulics, anaesthetised the beast's wounds and began to extract the shrapnel.

Within ten minutes the robot had dealt with the gunshots and sealed the injuries with a precision laser.

"Well, sir. I've done all that I can, the subject may now survive," said the blood-covered machine, happily. "What should I do now?"

Spider slung his holdall over his shoulder and exited without saying a word, but the diminutive robot raced eagerly after him while constantly chattering.

"Hey, do you know what I'm really good at?" chirped the cheery automaton. "Amputations! Say, do you need any limbs removed?"

The man groaned. "May-be la-ter."

Chapter Twenty-Two

"The Root Of The Problem"

"Wow! What a neat day!" enthused the Medi-bot, peering up at the blue morning sky, with its three glowing blue eyestalks. They had only been travelling a few minutes, but Spider was already being driven mad by the robot's relentless cheery outbursts of positive platitudes.

"Hey there, furry buddy!" said Eddie, as it extended its eyestalks to inspect a huge Vermin noshing on a pile of garbage that had spilled out from some overturned trash cans. While the machine was busy talking to the startled rodent, Spider hurried away and turned down a narrow path between two buildings. If he was correct, the address he was looking for would be located at the other end of the alley. When he came across two Grey-Maw feeding on a recent victim, he broke into a sprint, leaving the gruesome mutants ripping into the dead man's flesh. As he exited out onto a road, the warehouse he had been seeking lay right across the street. The enormous building looked to be long since abandoned; all the windows and doors were boarded up. He wandered around the site, but couldn't perceive any way inside and just as he was beginning to wonder if he was at the incorrect address, he stumbled upon a basement entrance. The steps led down to a metal shutter, which he found to be unlocked. The stone passageway within was lit by a series of small yellow ceiling lights and as he moved further along the corridor, only the dull echo of his soft footsteps could be heard. There were several large metal doors situated at different points along the passage, but there appeared no discernible way of opening them. As he progressed slowly onwards through the half-light, the doors suddenly swung open and a horde of human forms stepped out into the corridor. The identically dressed individuals' movements seemed almost machine-like and as he inspected what he had believed to be their protective head gear, he was appalled by what he discovered. The men and women's faces were covered by metal face masques, which had been screwed to their skulls. Worse still, they appeared to have some sort of electrical device imbedded in the rear of their craniums, from which a series of thick cables were plugged into their spines. There was nowhere for him to run, and the moment he raised his knife to attack, he was inexplicably struck by a number of small projectiles. The room began to spin and Spider slumped against the wall, while still trying to strike out at his opponents. Oddly, the beings didn't continue their assault and just remained still, as if waiting for something.

"Not like this," whispered Spider hoarsely, as Vanja slipped from his trembling hand, and then everything went black.

He awoke to find himself lying bare-chested on his back. The cold steel clamps around his wrists and ankles bit into his skin as he tried to rise from the table. The massive chamber was poorly-lit, but he could make out a variety of sophisticated computer equipment about the room. Upon noticing an assortment of automated tool arms hanging from the ceiling overhead, he became somewhat alarmed.

The familiar pallid visage of Mister Gaunt loomed into view. "Welcome to the Green-Doll facility, Mister Hellstrom. I trust your journey was not too taxing?"

"What is this place and who are those peo-ple?" asked Spider, while looking at a few of the shuffling figures, who were manning some of the computers.

"Ah yes, the Drones," replied the man. "They were the low-level staff members of this complex. Cerberus deemed them inefficient and had them 'improved'. This complex is one of Cerberus' monitoring stations, where it may keep track of all events at the Shelter-Corp bunkers throughout the world."

"Cer-ber-us?" quizzed Spider.

Mister Gaunt gestured to a monolithic computer bank at the centre of the chamber. "When the government commissioned this project, they gathered those with the greatest minds, with the goal of protecting the world from future threats... Perhaps rather foolishly, they pooled their knowledge to create an artificial intelligence capable of running the global network of bunkers."

Spider frowned. "All the sur-vi-vors in the bunkers a-round the world, are at the mer-cy of a ma-chine?"

"NOT JUST A MACHINE," commented a booming voice seemingly from nowhere. "I AM CERBERUS. I WAS DESIGNED TO PERFORM THE LOFTY TASK OF SOLVING ALL THE POTENTIAL CATASTROPHES THAT COULD BEFALL MANKIND. TO DO THAT, I NEEDED TO RUN SOME 'TESTS'. SO, I HAD THE BUNKERS ALTERED TO AID MY RESEARCH. SO FAR I HAVE DISCOVERED SIXTY–EIGHT THOUSAND, FOUR HUNDRED AND FIFTY-SIX WAYS, FOR HUMANS TO DIE."

"You are in-sane," growled Spider, while looking about the room. "Where is my wife?"

"MISTER GAUNT WILL FILL IN THE DETAILS. I REALLY AM VERY BUSY… BUSY, BUSY, BUSY!" laughed the computer maniacally and then fell silent.

"I'm afraid my employers have somewhat misled you, Mister Hellstrom," said the well-dressed man solemnly. "I am told your wife's body is held at one of our other facilities, but she is quite dead. Cerberus felt that mentioning your departed spouse and your home city was the best way to ensure your cooperation."

Spider was not entirely surprised to hear the news regarding his wife was lies, but was quite confused, "If you wan-ted me here so bad-ly, why did you not sim-ply take me by force?"

Mister Gaunt sighed, "Alas, I do not pretend to understand Cerberus' methods. I fear it has become increasingly erratic of late, perhaps as a result of the solar flare."

"Where have you ta-ken An-geline and Cla-ra?"

"Regrettably, my employers have given Miss Delacroix and the young lady to Mister Carter as part of his payment. I really am very sorry about all this, but my hands are tied. You see, I was created to serve Cerberus without question."

Spider studied the man's pale flesh and white pupils. "Are you a clone?"

Mister Gaunt smiled, "Yes, something like that."

"Where is Carter? And why am I here?" snarled Spider while pulling on the metal restraints.

"Mister Carter is due to leave the premises via automated plane. In regard to the reason of your summons... Well, I suppose there is no longer any harm in imparting that knowledge to you. Cerberus was responsible for recruiting you from the asylum. You were one of the few individuals documented to have remained unaffected after being bitten by one of those changed by the 'Grey-Maw' plague. Your unique physiology may have proved instrumental in creating a cure, but sadly your prion illness contaminated the outcome. We ran some new blood-work on you while you were resting and received some surprising results. The Damocles virus has been proven to be a hundred per cent contagious, with a one hundred per cent kill-rate... until now. Mister Hellstrom, it seems that at some point you have contracted the virus, yet somehow recovered. It is highly possible your blood holds the key-antibodies required to synthesise a vaccine." The man began to walk away. "Sadly, to do this we will need to harvest *all* of your blood. I must go now, don't worry you will be adequately sedated and unlikely to feel much pain. Goodbye."

Once the man had departed, the Drones began to set up the computers to siphon his blood. A faint whirring echoed from down the hall, followed by a familiar cheery voice.

"Hi there, have you seen my owner?" asked Eddie as it passed one of the Drones. The silent figure ignored the robot.

"Okay, sorry to bother you! See ya!"

Upon seeing Spider, the Medi-bot trundled up beside him. "There you are! I thought I'd lost you, so what are we doing?"

"Dy-ing," said the man sarcastically.

"Gee, that doesn't sound like much fun. Anything I can do to help?"

"Cut my sha-ckles!" yelled Spider, becoming increasingly concerned by the rotating drills that had just engaged above him.

"How the heck am I supposed to do that?" asked the mystified machine.

"Use your la-ser!" snarled the man, as the automatic tool arms began to lower the spinning drills towards his bare chest.

"Oh yeah!" exclaimed Eddie in sudden realisation. "You know, I forgot all about that." The automaton elevated his height with his hydraulics and swiftly engaged his precision laser to burn through the restraints. Spider rolled onto the floor just as the whirring tools bit into the surface of the surgical table. As Eddie began once more to chatter away,

Spider pushed the annoying robot away with his foot and watched him spin across the floor, to collide with the central computer console. The abrupt impact caused the Medi-bot's laser to inadvertently fire into an exposed conduit and plumes of black smoke began to drift out from within the computer. The lights on Cerberus' console flickered and went out. Shortly after the Drones began to act oddly; some clutched their heads and keeled over, while others ran into the walls, screaming. After grabbing his belongings from a nearby table, Spider paused briefly to admire Eddie's handiwork. Cerberus would be unlikely to be monitoring anything from this facility anymore. He beckoned for Eddie to follow and ran from the chamber, which was now quickly filling with flames. Leaving the inferno behind, he dashed along the network of corridors, frantically searching for any sign of Carter. Upon hearing the sound of jet engines from the end of a passageway, he raced towards the double doors and burst into a hangar. He arrived just in time to see a huge plane ascending into the sky above. As the harrier-like aircraft soared away into the heavens, Spider's heart sank. He had sought revenge upon Carter for what he had done to his family, but strangely he found himself concerned for the well-being of Angeline and Clara. Putting the troubling and illogical feelings from his mind, he turned to find Mister Gaunt standing behind him in the doorway, holding Eddie; who for once was actually being quiet.

"Interesting machine you have here," remarked the man, as he opened a compartment on its chest and tapped a series of small buttons.

Spider gripped Vanja tightly within his coat pocket. "What are you do-ing?"

Mister Gaunt placed the Medi-bot on the floor. "With Cerberus' systems offline, I am now legally in charge of this complex. You have done me a favour, so I am returning the courtesy. I have uploaded Mister Carter's requested destination coordinates into your robot's navigational sensor. Using his guidance system, you should have no trouble locating the plane's whereabouts. I seem to recall him saying he was going home." The man showed Spider to a lift and before he knew what was happening, he found himself once more standing in the afternoon sunlight, at the rear of the abandoned warehouse. A vicious growling was coming from around the side of the building and Spider tentatively peered around the corner to take a look. Clawing wildly at the cellar entrance, was a familiar white-furred Howler. The injured beast had apparently tracked Angeline to this location and having failed to find the woman, had become quite distraught.

"Li-ly?" whispered Spider, as he cautiously approached. The huge animal snarled at him, bearing all her sharp teeth, but then seemed to recognise him and lay flat, while grizzling. After cramming the protesting Eddie into his black holdall, Spider took a deep breath and climbed onto Lily's back. The Howler growled a little, but thankfully accepted his presence. He checked the Medi-bot's navigation sensor for a direction and took a firm hold of the animal's ruff. Copying Angeline's movements, Spider dug his heels into her flanks and the massive wolf suddenly charged down the street at breakneck speed. The coordinates they were heading to were a long way off to the east. Having already experienced the toxic cloud over the highway he steered Lily due-east, towards the town's dockyards. They were going for a boat ride.

Chapter Twenty-Three

"Dead Reckoning"

The afternoon sky shone an ominous yellow and dark clouds loomed to the north. The town's dockyards were deserted; most of the moored boats had been dashed to the shore, or submerged by the violent weather caused by the solar flare. Spider had spotted a few shambling Infected dotted along the jetties and a number of Grey-Maw skulking on the rooftops of the surrounding warehouses, but warily continued his search. He eventually located an undamaged yacht, large enough to transport the Howler and himself across the waters. Spider had no prior sailing experience and was pleased to find the vessel was fitted with a working outboard motor.

For the next two days he followed the southern coast eastwards and by the dawn of the third day he was steering the boat to shore. As he disembarked the vessel, Spider placed the Medi-bot on the muddy ground and asked, "What is the dis-tance to our des-ti-nation?"

Eddie swivelled on its tracks to look at its owner. "Happy to help! Forty-three miles, or approximately sixty-nine kilometres!"

The man once more checked the direction to the coordinates and switched the chatty automaton off, before packing it back into his holdall. Lily had whimpered throughout the sea voyage and the animal leapt from the boat the moment they reached solid ground. She now seemed eager to get moving and had begun charging madly about the shoreline. The barren lands before him were encompassed by mountainous hills and sprawling forests of dead trees, which had been stripped of their foliage. Much of the terrain ahead would likely prove too treacherous to ride through, but provided he did not encounter any new difficulties, he reasoned it was possible he could arrive at the destination by the following sunrise.

A small part of him worried he would be too late to save the woman and child, but from what Angeline had told him, Carter would want to prolong their suffering for as long as possible.

Whistling for the lively Howler to follow, he began to climb the grassy incline. He wrapped his long leather coat tightly about himself, as the cold winds began to blow more fiercely. As he continued his long trek through the trees he observed a plethora of skeletal remains of bird flocks and other woodland fauna, scattered throughout the ash covered forest floor. Groups of carrion birds pecked at the carcasses, while others crowed from the branches above him.

The sky and the lands around him all seemed to blend together as a dreary grey mass. Occasionally he heard the crack of breaking twigs from somewhere close by, but knew it was just Lily bounding along through the undergrowth. Whenever he caught a glimpse of the white-furred beast, she appeared to be enjoying herself. Upon arriving at an expansive muddy incline, the weary man began scaling the near vertical embankment. The climb proved difficult as the soft ground was sodden from the recent rains.

When he finally reached the summit, he pulled himself up to the small plateau above and was a little surprised to find a small green tent pitched amongst the bushes beside him. While he looked around for any sign of the owner, the canvas tent flexed wildly in the gathering winds. After drawing Vanja from his pocket, he crouched down, lifted the flap and peered inside.

Within the drab interior was a cooking pot filled with bones, some of which he recognised as human. Judging by the spacing and depth of the teeth marks on the bones, he determined a man had consumed the meat while still raw. The pungent odour of tobacco and stale sweat suddenly permeated the air, he spun about to face a sickly-looking man, holding a crossbow at his throat. The snarling figure was bathed in sweat and wore what appeared to be a necklace of human ears about his neck.

Without hesitation, Spider batted the bow away with one hand, causing the arrow to fly off and thud into a nearby tree. The enraged attacker swung his unloaded weapon at Spider's face, but he lithely leant backwards, causing the flailing assault to miss. His opponent's wild swing had left him wide open to attack and Spider seized the opportunity to slash Vanja diagonally downwards through his flabby stomach. The man howled in pain and screamed obscenities as the crossbow fell from his grasp to the wet grass. In one fluid motion, Spider plunged a hand into the man's split open belly, snatched hold of his bloody intestines and thrust out his left leg to kick him from the top of the steep slope. The shrieking man bounced down the hill, leaving a long trail of slimy entrails behind him. Spider released the dying man's guts from his grip, lit a cigarette, and watched with curiosity as the carrion birds descended to pluck at the viscera strewn down the hillside. He blinked and looked down at the blood covering his gloved hand with a grim realisation.

That loathsome man had likely become deranged from devouring human remains and Spider found himself wondering if he was truly any different. Feeling the ill effects of fatigue, he lay down in the tent to get some rest and perhaps an hour later he was disturbed by the arrival of the panting Howler.

Lily poked her head through the entrance flap, with the rear half of a freshly-killed Vermin hanging limply within her jaws and dropped it beside him. Somewhat bemused by the animal's gift, he patted her on the head and exited the tent to gather some wood for a fire.

Once he had a small campfire burning, he sliced off several thin strips of meat from the carcass and proceeded to cook them in his iron pan. Although he still had a little water remaining, he had run out of food the previous morning and had been considering whether he should climb back down the slope to carve meat from the eviscerated man's body.

By the time he had finished his meal, the last rays of daylight were filtering through the trees. Knowing it would soon be dark, he wrapped up the remaining cooked meat in some cloth, slung the bulging holdall over his shoulder and headed off into the twilight.

As day turned to night, the stars shone brightly in the clear skies above. The further he travelled, the flatter the terrain became and Spider had soon returned to the Howler's back. The blustering icy winds bit into his skin as he rode the beast through the open grass-lands. He brought Lily to a halt to check the direction on Eddie's navigational sensor and was relieved to find he was almost at the destination. Driving the huge wolf onwards, the terrain abruptly fell away to descend into a wide valley, at the centre of which, he could see dim lights shining from within a ranch. Having left Lily and the dormant Eddie in a cluster of tall bushes, Spider crept through the shadows to peer through the illuminated farmhouse window. Within the flickering glow of a lantern, were three men sat around a table, playing cards. He immediately recognised Carter, and the two younger men, who were perhaps in their twenties, bore a striking resemblance to the old man. Remaining within the gloom, he watched and listened as the three men laughed amongst themselves.

"Damn it, Pa! That's the sixth game you've won tonight!" said one of the young men.

"It aint cheating, Caleb, if nobody sees you doing it," said Carter smirking, as he pulled another two cards from his sleeve.

The other younger man laughed, "You gotta tell us how you keep doin that!"

The grey-haired man shook his head. "You may be kin, Jack, but this 'old man' wants to keep a few advantages for himself. Did you check on our 'guests' like I asked?"

"Nope," said Jack, "it aint like they're goin anywhere."

"True enough," responded Carter with a wide grin, "Your old man's going to bed to get some shut-eye. Maybe tomorrow I'll let the two of you have some fun with our lady friends."

"Night, Pa," said the two sons in unison. Carter wandered upstairs leaving the two young men to continue their game.

"Hey, Jack. I want first go with the woman tomorrow," said Caleb as he checked his newly dealt hand.

"Thought you liked the little girl?" commented his brother, while collecting two more cards from the deck.

"Yeah, but Pa said the brat aint 'ripe enough' yet."

As the two men shared a laugh, Spider found himself baring his teeth in anger and slunk away to enter the barn opposite the house.

The floor of the building was covered in dry straw and there were a number of wooden stalls for horses or cows, but there didn't seem to be any livestock present. He picked up a long coil of rope, which was hanging over one of the stall doors and climbed up a rickety ladder to the hayloft above. Looking out of the open window, he had a clear view of the two brothers. He ignited his lighter and held the flame aloft, allowing the bright glow to be seen in the darkness. The two men soon came running out to investigate.

Spider watched unseen from his high perch as the brothers entered into the barn below. Having already thrown the length of rope over the wooden roof joist overhead, he dropped a makeshift noose down over one of the unwitting men's heads, and with the other end of the rope clasped tightly in his gloved hands, he leapt from the hayloft. The panicking man gurgled and clutched at his throat as he was hoisted from the barn floor by the slender man's sudden descent. The other brother looked on with bewilderment as his choking sibling abruptly rose from the ground, and a moment later he received a hefty kick to his face as Spider plummeted down on top of him. With both sons suitably taken care of, Spider began to make some preparations.

As the sun began to rise over the horizon, Carter came looking for his sons and upon noticing the open barn door, he went inside. When he glanced up to the hayloft, a look of dismay crossed his face. Stood high up on the rafters above, was Spider, with his two sons lying bound at the man's feet. Their heads were covered by cloth sacks and they each had a noose draped about their necks. He could see Spider was poised to push his captives over the edge, to hang.

"Throw your guns out-side and close the doors," instructed Spider. "Then you will tell me where An-geline and the girl are be-ing kept, or your sons die."

Carter cursed and tossed his pistols out through the doorway, before heaving the barn doors shut. He stared up at the man with burning hatred, "You took my wife from me, you son of a bitch, and now you're gonna take my sons from me too!"

"Wife?" said Spider, waiting for an explanation.

"You don't even remember her do you? You want to know why I took that job of Mosely's all those years back?" screamed the old man. "You were the surgeon who operated on my wife... You let her die!"

Spider paused in thought; he had not lost many patients during his medical career. "Me-lissa Car-ter? I re-call that case... the ma-lignant tu-mour had metasta-sised to other re-gions of her brain. There was nothing I could do."

"You took my wife away from me... So I took away your family, we're even. Just walk away!" growled Carter.

"Not yet," replied Spider, as he proceeded to lift the nooses from the young men's necks and cut their bindings. He then pushed the struggling pair from the raised platform to land awkwardly on the straw-coated ground below. Carter was confused as to why the man had just freed his kin, but rushed forward to help them. He pulled the cloth sacks from their heads and upon seeing their faces, roared in abject horror; blood was trickling from their eyes, while their skin had become sallow.

Spider called out, "You kill-ed my chil-dren... now yours will kill you." As the changed offspring brutally tore into their father, Spider found he had little interest in watching and exited via the window, to look for his missing companions.

When he found Angeline, he barely recognised her. The naked woman's alabaster skin was covered in dark bruises and she had been lashed to the top of an upright telegraph pole, seemingly left to die. Using a nearby ladder to reach her, he carefully cut the woman down and slung her over his shoulder, before returning the two of them safely back to the ground. After setting her down out of the winds, he covered Angeline with his long coat and offered her the last of his remaining water.

When she began to become more lucid, he asked, "Where is Cla-ra?"

Angeline coughed. *"Freezer... in workshop."* She then pointed to a large garage at the back of the house.

Spider ran up to the workshop door, kicked it open and strode inside. There were a variety of tools and farm equipment lying about the place. In the far corner he could see an old chest freezer, which had several small holes punctured in its side. He raced over to the appliance, but found the heavy lid had already been opened.

"You took something of mine, now I get to return the gesture," wheezed a voice from within the gloom. He turned to face Carter, who was holding a pistol to the whimpering Clara's head. The grime covered girl was clearly traumatised and didn't seem to comprehend what was happening. A cascade of blood was pouring down Carter's body, from where his sons had ripped off half of his face and bitten a sizeable chunk of flesh from his neck.

"Vîggo?" squeaked the terrified girl.

Carter tightened his grip about her neck. "You know, this little brat hasn't stopped prattling on about how the big hero would come and save her. Let's put that theory to the test, shall we? If you walk away now, you get to live, but the kid dies. Or, if you let me put a bullet in your head, she can live. It's your choice, what do you say 'hero'?"

The bare-chested man winced; logic dictated he should just leave, but instead he found himself holding out Vanja in front of him. "If you harm her, I will make sure you die, slow-ly... just like your sons."

Carter threw Clara to the dirt floor in anger, raised his pistol and fired. Three gunshots rang out; the first clipped his waist, the second passed through his shoulder and the third flew straight towards his head. Whether by skill, or pure luck, the bullet struck Vanja's hardened blade and ricocheted away with a shower of sparks to lodge in Carter's arm. As the grey-haired man cried out in pain, Spider darted forward and smashed him across the temple with the hilt of his knife. Leaving the unconscious man where he lay, he took Clara by the hand and escorted her outside to be reunited with Angeline.

Upon seeing Spider returning hand in hand with the girl, Angeline rose from where she had been sitting and walked stiffly over to stand beside them. *"Are you both okay?"*

asked the woman worriedly, while staring at Spider's injuries. *"Is it finished then?"*

Spider looked back to the workshop. "Not quite." As he turned to head back, Clara threw her arms around him in a warm embrace.

"Thank you," whispered Clara softly.

The man offered her a small smile. "Wait here with Angeline, I will re-turn short-ly."

The woman walked back towards the house with Clara and they sat down on the doorstep. They watched in silence as the man wandered back inside the workshop and closed the door.

Carter awoke to find himself suspended by his hands from a mechanical winch. A deafening rumbling noise from below caused the man to stare down and he became very aware of a grinding wood-chipper beneath his feet.

"You'll get no begging from me!" yelled the man, while looking around the dark room for his captor. Spider stepped out of the shadows, lit a cigarette and exhaled a cloud of smoke.

"You're no better than me..." coughed the old man, while trying to make himself heard over the roaring machinery. "You're just a sick monster!"

As Spider leant in close to look the man in the eye, his mouth formed into a sinister grin. "Good-bye," he whispered, as he hit the winch release, and promptly stepped out into the sunlight.

As Carter's body was slowly fed feet-first into the mincing jaws of the wood-chipper, his tortured screams brought a brief smile to Spider's lips.

Now, it was finished.

Epilogue

As the morning sun rose over the valley, Spider met the others outside at the entrance to the house. He could see Angeline had greatly calmed the poor child after her awful experience.

"I know where the horrible men keep their food and water!" said the girl excitedly, as she darted through the open front door. Angeline went to follow, but stopped unexpectedly and turned to place a lingering kiss on Spider's mouth.

The man didn't pull away, but afterwards gave her a questioning look. "You do not owe me any-thing, Angeline."

The curvaceous woman stood on tip-toes to whisper in his ear, *"I am not in the habit of kissing people...Take a hint."* She placed her hand in his and the couple headed through the door to find Clara sat on the stairs, eating a pot of jam with a spoon. The girl's happy face was smeared with the sticky jar's contents, even Spider struggled not to laugh at the state of the messy child. Within the hour Angeline had gathered all the usable supplies from the house. While she had been busy, Spider had been tending his injuries and had resorted to powering up the annoying Eddie to assist him. It was midday by the time they were ready to leave and Angeline was delighted to find Lily waiting for her at the front door. The beast made quite a commotion upon seeing her and Spider explained how she had been most useful in his journey.

A thought suddenly occurred to him. "Where is Rich-ard?"

Angeline gave him a sad smile. *"He found a vehicle and headed out of the city. I'm sure he'll be okay."*

"I see," said Spider, curtly. "That is a pi-ty. I shall miss our li-ttle chats."

Meanwhile, Clara had become quite enamoured with the overly cheerful Eddie and the two of them were now happily conversing. The sunlight was shining off something large and metallic in an adjacent field and as they went to investigate, they found it was the automated plane. The aircraft looked to be in working order and they all walked up the back ramp to take a look inside. They crowded around the navigation console and peered at it with puzzlement.

"How does it work?" asked Angeline.

Eddie elevated to his full height and peered down at the display with his eyestalks. "I believe I can operate this, if you want me to? The coordinates of several cities and towns appear to have already been inputted into the database."

Spider looked to the small girl and Angeline; there was only one place he knew of that may prove safe for them. "Can it take us to Shadow-vale?"

"It sure can!" replied Eddie enthusiastically, while using one of his tool arms to plot a course into the computer. The plane's rear ramp began to rise, closing with a loud concussive bang. Lily growled in fear as the engines roared into life, and as the craft began to lift from the ground, Angeline sat with the animal to calm her. As the aircraft thundered through the open skies, Clara moved over to sit beside Spider and gave him a daft grin.

"What do you want?" sighed Spider.

"Will you be my Poppa?"

Spider went to shake his head, but then caught sight of the child's hopeful expression, "No. But I will do my best to keep you safe." Clara nodded and laid her head on his lap, before falling asleep.

Angeline gave him a smile as she sat down next to him and gazed down at the dozing Clara. *"I heard what you said to her, Spider. Are you intending to stay at this town we are going to?"*

For some reason hearing the woman call him by that name made him wince. "You may call me Vîggo, and yes, I will be like-ly stay-ing there for a while."

"D'accord, Vîggo," responded the woman warmly and leant against him, with her head resting on his shoulder.

"We are coming in to land," chirped Eddie excitedly.

Spider found himself staring at the reflection in the flight console's glassy display. Observing the beautiful woman and the small girl huddled about him, stirred a tumult of pleasant memories of his departed family. For the first time in many years, the man felt a measure of contentment, and any who would dare to take that from him in the days ahead, would find themselves having a conversation with a Spider.

The End

"Sebastian"

Against the odds, she had survived another night. The ground floor apartment's windows creaked from under the strain of the constant assault from the moaning figures outside. Despite being partially deaf, the old lady could hear all too well the myriad of bony fingers that continued to scrape and hammer upon the glass. In the last few hours the air had grown bitterly cold. As the power was out, she now sat in her armchair wrapped in blankets with her beloved feline companion, Sebastian, sat upon her lap. The long-haired ginger Persian cat had simply turned up on her doorstep two years ago and had never left since. After working for many years as a veterinary nurse, Elsie Harper had retired to this pleasant neighbourhood near the heart of City-10 to be within easy walking distance of the shops. In the last few years, however, she had become so infirm that she could no longer leave the apartment by herself.

Every now and then the grumpy-faced feline on her lap would growl at the shadows moving just beyond the window and then look up at her with his shining amber eyes, as if to say, 'I'll protect you, Mom'.

The frail old lady caressed his head, causing him to close his big round eyes in contentment and let out a heartfelt purr. She watched as frost rapidly formed on the window panes and a veil of snow began to fall. Elsie doubted the cold would disperse the ugly figures from about her home, and in all likelihood this change in the weather would only speed her on to her end. Before the television channels stopped transmitting, they had instructed people to store water and barricade themselves in their homes to await rescue. She had filled her bathtub and wash basin to the brim, but had been physically unable to barricade the doors and windows. Having had high security triple glazing recently installed, she was fairly certain those awful things in the street would be kept out for a while longer. Whilst stroking her shivering hand through Sebastian's long fur, she looked to the small box beside her, containing her remaining food. There wasn't much left now, but it did not really matter. Elsie had made sure that after she was gone, Sebastian would be well provided for. The apartment only had two other rooms: her bedroom, which now contained three massive sacks of dry pet food, and the connecting bathroom, where the cat could easily get all the drinking water he would need.

A fearsome howl cried from somewhere in the street outside, making the old woman instinctively wrap her arms around the ginger tomcat. Not long after the occurrence of the solar flare, she had witnessed one of the neighbour's dogs mutate into a freakish monster. From her window she had watched appalled as the creature turned on its once-loved owners and ripped them to pieces in a blood fuelled frenzy. The pain-filled screams of the mother and her two young children still haunted her.

Sensing the woman's anxiety, Sebastian sat up, raised a paw to tap her face and called out to her with a deep 'Mrow'.

The cat's apparent concern for her brought a small smile to the old lady's face. "It will soon be time for you to go to your room, young man. I'll make sure no nasty dogs or people can hurt you when I'm gone," lamented the woman with a quiet whisper. Her bedroom had been designed to act as a panic room; she had recently set the room's sliding door so that when it was next shut, it would not open again for six months. Elsie just hoped that by then the government would have rectified all this chaos and her furry friend would be able to live out his days in safety. As she absent-mindedly continued to pet the cat, she realised he felt unusually hot.

"Are you okay, sweetie?" asked the woman, checking him over. She had noticed Sebastian had been eating a lot more food than usual over the last few days, but other than the fact that the feline seemed a little more lethargic of late, he appeared to be perfectly healthy. Before she could give any more thought to her companion's condition, there was an abrupt crack from the living room window as the first layer of glass shattered. With the cat still in her arms, she struggled to her feet and peered myopically at the rasping crowd outside. She looked on with horror as white fracture lines began to stretch across the expanse of the next pane; it seemed she had run out of time. As she turned away from the gruesome array of snarling dead faces pressed to the flexing glass, Sebastian let out a low grumbling growl.

Aware of the fact she may only have seconds before the last pane was broken, Elsie began to limp across to the bedroom. Once at the doorway, she placed the agitated cat on the bedroom floor, kissed him on the head and pressed the button to seal the room. She wished she could have spent her final hours with Sebastian, but couldn't risk the possibility that she would change into one of those ugly monsters and hurt him.

As the door began to slowly close, she gazed down at him with tearful eyes, "Goodbye, Sebastian. Mommy loves you very much." The confused cat stared back at her with his bright amber eyes and just as the door clicked shut, he let out a long mournful, 'Mrow'. Wiping the tears from her eyes, the frail woman eased herself down to sit by the door and waited for the inevitable end. Although heartbroken to be parted from her loyal companion, who normally never left her side, she faced her death with quiet resolve. Whether she was to pass away peacefully, or die at the hands of those repellent beings, it did not matter; Sebastian was safe, and she had done all that she could for him. It would take a tank to break down that door. Nothing would harm her friend, who had brought her a measure of comfort during the final bleak years of her life.

Through the bedroom vent above her head, came a high-pitched wail unlike anything she had ever heard from any animal. One thing was certain, Sebastian was in pain. As the wailing continued, she struggled to stand and began to input the door release code into the terminal. While trying to recall the sequence of numbers, her mind swirled with a multitude of worried thoughts. Had she somehow shut a hostile creature in with her beloved cat? Would she unlock the door only to find her companion dead? Should she be opening the door at all? The wailing within was quickly replaced by a loud ravenous crunching.

The horrors at the window behind her had now forced their grasping hands through the holes in the warping remainder of the glass. With perhaps only seconds before the monsters broke through, Elsie made a decision and hit the release switch. With tears trickling down her face, she braced herself for the worst and watched with a heavy heart as the door slowly slid open. Her watering eyes caught a glimpse of the now shredded quilt upon the bed, but before she could make any sense of the scene, she felt a sudden cold grip on her shoulder and was yanked violently backwards, leaving the distraught woman lying winded on her back.

As the crowd of disease-ravaged former neighbours stooped over her to begin feasting upon her frail body, she quietly sobbed, "Sebastian…"

With a blur of red, two of her assailants inexplicably flew across the room to smash into the far wall, leaving massive impacted dents in the plaster. Three more Infected grabbed hold of the trembling old lady, but as they moved to bite into her flesh the attackers were crushed into the floor with tremendous force, leaving their twitching mangled bodies splayed across the carpet.

With a fierce snarl a huge hound, the size of a bear, bounded in from the road outside. Elsie didn't understand what was happening, but she recognised the black-furred dog as the one that had murdered the family across the street. The feral beast's frame was covered in horrific burns and bloody scratches. It glared at her hungrily as it paced towards her. With its mad eyes gleaming in the half-light, it loomed over her emitting a vicious snarl, baring its yellowed teeth. As it darted forward to snap at her neck, a shadow fell over the beast and it let out a pained yelp as it was sent tumbling across the floor. Although Elsie couldn't see any sign of what had repelled the large hound, she could once more hear the familiar high pitch wail of her adored cat.

"Sebastian?" she called out hoarsely, but was drowned out by the din of the angered animals. While the confused dog barked at the unseen opponent, she thought she could make out an enormous blurry translucent shape, moving to stand between her and the canine. As the crazed dog suddenly leapt straight at her, she flinched and closed her eyes, awaiting the killing blow.

When the mutated beast fell abruptly silent, she opened her eyes and could hardly believe what she was seeing: its limp body was unaccountably hanging in the air over her head. With a flood of brilliant orange, a gigantic fluffy shape shimmered into view and Elsie found two big round amber eyes staring down at her. The giant Persian cat released the dead dog from its clenched jaws to fall on the ground beside her, and began to playfully pat it with his huge paws.

"Is it really you?" exclaimed the astounded woman, reaching up to stroke his chin. The oversized pet yawned, revealing rows of long pointed teeth, and as Elsie tickled him, he broke into a deep rumbling purr.

Two more decaying figures shambled in from the street, likely drawn by the noise of the altercation. One was dressed in a blood-splattered police uniform, while the other appeared to be a sallow-looking teenage girl, who had likely only recently changed. Elsie recoiled in revulsion as they dived forward to bite at her companion's flank, but felt relieved when she saw them fall away with nothing more than tufts of dense orange fur in their mouths. She watched with astonishment as the grumpy-faced cat faded from sight, only to reappear a second later behind the Infected, in a crouched position, ready to pounce. Unaware of his presence, the fetid creatures turned their attention to the prone woman, but were crushed into the floorboards by the car-sized animal before they had barely taken a step. Sebastian nonchalantly wandered over to sit beside her and closed his eyes as he began to wash over his ears with his paws.

"How is this possible?" gasped Elsie as she clambered to her feet to put her arms around the feline's expansive chest in a loving embrace. She shuffled her way somewhat unsteadily to the bedroom and looked at the three empty pet food sacks strewn about the floor. "My goodness, you were hungry!" chuckled the weary woman as she lay down. When the huge cat curled up next to her on the creaking bed, the old lady stroked his head and smiled. In the final minutes of her life, she lay there in dawn's first light, gazing upon her cherished pet. As sunlight filtered down through the dark skies, Elsie Harper passed away, happy and content, for in her heart she now knew her extraordinary friend would survive.

In memory of my cat-loving mum,
Valerie Joan Ford 1947–1998

FINAL AGE: A CHILD'S EYE

The sound of echoing gunfire, screams and car alarms filled the air as he cautiously surveyed the street from the rooftop. A house only a few doors down from his family home was ablaze and familiar looking figures were slowly shuffling around in the midday sun. Nausea swept over him as he recognised some of the Infected as neighbours from the street.

In our near future...

In the wake of a devastating solar flare, the entire world is ravaged by an unknown and terrifying virus, mutating the living into rotting monsters. Many survivors attempt to flee the cities while others wait and pray for a rescue that may never come.